Cadillac

MW01205765

To en
create

B. R. Cook
2-11-12

RESET

BY MARIAN EVANS

BY BRIAN COOL

ILLUSTRATIONS BY STEVE MANN

ISBN-10: 1463599560

ISBN-13: 978-1463599560

CONTENTS

for the girl that was George Eliot

My Dear Reader,

Welcome to MY world–to catch a phrase that you Earthlings use so readily, carelessly–she is Aerda, far out there amongst the lonely stars tonight. May she rest in peace. She deserves it certainly. This story, told from the perspective of one who barely lived through it, tells of the momentous occurrence that changed everything about the life we knew there.

How I was propelled to here, from there, across the blank black reaches of space, which the Far Seers call *the mind of God*–on a silver stream of consciousness–I don't completely understand, but here I am. Here to wonder and hopefully learn, here to witness bear, as in the following, and here to tell.

How I came to Earth isn't really what I ponder anyway; it's "why?" Why me . . . why now, and to what possible end?

Sometimes I try to tell myself, that it's all just a big cosmic accident, like the face on Mars or the Byzantine batteries, and it may yet prove to be. Other times, I think that perhaps *they* finally got me after all, and that this fair Earth is the final strange dream of my dying brain.

Then it goes on . . . and on . . . . Past all hope of reasoning away.

As long as it does, let me tell you the things I've heard on the winds of Aerda. This was the last, the end–there's nothing like starting at the finish line–and now I find that some energetic connection, tenuous on Aerda, has been broken on Earth.

The early part of the story that follows was unfolding around me, when my life essence was–for lack of a better word–*transported* here, into the tangled mind of this earthly human host. Given what I know, and could logically infer, and using a gram of imagination, I conceived the ending. I wouldn't make up such a hopeful thing just to comfort myself, I believe it is as probable an ending, as it is a truthful beginning. If there are lessons to learn from what follows, it depends on whether the fates of different worlds are somehow intertwined.

The main character is an old friend, Wilhelmina Walker. I met her during the summer I spent at a camp for troubled young girls, years ago on the Altalanta. She was different–for some reason I couldn't hear her thoughts, and I quickly grew to like that, and her because of it. We made a solemn pact to look each other up when we could. We sealed it with our blood, as in the days of old. I guess the world got in our way.

Do I miss her now, my world? I surely wish I could. What I do miss is what she might have been. By the time I left, *or was taken*, I had no family, no friends, no home. Half starving, haunted and hunted, I was much like the rebellious young lady in this story. But is Earth any better? For me, I have yet to decide. They are so like each other in many good respects, but also, in far too many wicked ways.

Like you, we had our Messiahs and our superstars, our world wars and our serial killers, our planes, trains, and automobiles. Our calendar was a bit off from yours, the day being a few minutes longer, the year being a couple days shorter. The climate, ratio of water to landmass, diversity of life forms, the planet's age and stage of evolutionary development, etc.; all similar to Earth's.

The languages of the two worlds are wholly different, but the people's thoughts are much the same, as far as I can see. By chance only, some of the words sound similar, just as some of my people could pass for Earth's–until the DNA tests, of course.

Many of the plants and animals of my world could also make it on Earth. So, part of me reasons that the key to why I was brought here, when the end came, was that I could fit in, if I would. Far from easy though, *fitting in*, no matter who you are, but I believe it is by that fact that I fit in here all the better.

In telling Willow's harrowing story, I rarely took the liberty of obscuring the differences between our planets. But bear with my use of certain English- or Earth-only phrases, or abbreviations. Where I've translated or quotated, my aim was to make sense, not to change the essential facts.

And forgive my penchant for fun where I had to adapt a few unpronounceable place names, like 'Narcsisippi'. I find it just as hard to wrap my tongue around some of your words like 'connectivity', as you might if trying the actual name for the mighty river Nrsowayosihp (which is about as close as I can come to spelling it in English).

Best regards, Marian

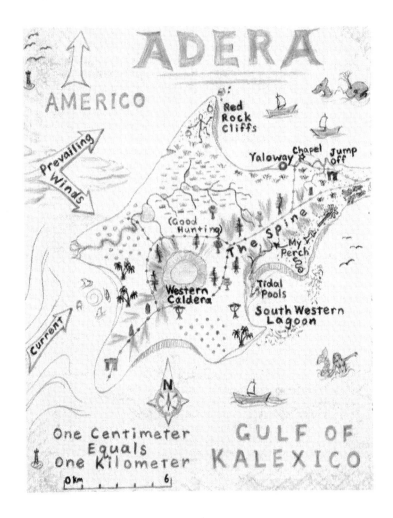

"The terrible great invisible eye of God never blinks–the empty infinite mind behind, never thinks." Maeva Endival

WILLOW AND THE ROCK GOD

Dusk. A grubby little green wooden boat was beached on the narrow spit of pale sand below me.

This was the easternmost tip of a semitropical islet–part of an old chain of volcanic islands. My spirit hovered like a lazy kite over the point of land, floating directly above a tall, dark, and precariously balanced construct of thick chunks of sea-worn shale.

Bloated purple clouds in a race south, lashed by thick whips of lightning, would carry their burden over the point, and yet a little further out to Mother Sea.

Whether blown ashore by salted breezes, dragged there by the tides, pulled by the force of gravity, or pushed there on the snouts of porpoises, this battered rowboat had caught the last possible stretch of beach before being swept further out to the merciless sea, and capsized in the south-going gale. A few late-flying seabirds veered away from the skiff, casting suspicious glances back as they came down to land a short ways to the west, near a pair of rotting right whale carcasses.

White rimmed waves toyed at the little boat, but seemed only to nudge it even further ashore. Lying as if thrown there, like some ragged discarded doll in the bottom of the boat, was the twisted body of a young woman. There was something hauntingly familiar about her, even from my point of view high overhead. She wore military boots, and several layers of thick clothing that had soaked up a good deal of water. Under her head, toward the prow, dried blood stained the floor of the boat. I watched her for a few minutes, looking in vain for some sign of life.

And there was something unsettling about the little rowboat. I'd seen it before somehow, somewhere, felt a connection to it. The craft's rugged little blue outboard leaned upside down in the prow. One end of a long nylon cord was tied around the shaft of the prop. The other end was lashed to a bracket on the nose of the boat. One of the oars was gone, missing from its socket. The other was locked in place, with the paddle end resting inside, pressed up against the young woman's waist.

It's me—

The body in the boat had my dark skin, my sooty black ringlets of shoulder length hair, my mannish chin, and my high cheekbones. *My blood.* I realized that the clothes were mine, stuff I'd scavenged along the way, mostly for its insulating value. It would be later before I would see the deep scabbed-over gashes up the left side of my neck and jaw.

I'd first thought of my floating consciousness as 'something new' when I had found myself, lighter than the wind, shimmering, draining upward, but it was the island that was new—to me at least.

There was no immediate sense of danger in my mind when I came to realize that I was looking down on my own body from a gull's-eye view. More than anything, I was amazed, except I couldn't see whether or not I was breathing. I found it strange to perceive the lightning and the last reddish tinges in the clouds on the western horizon, but neither hear the thunder, nor feel the howling winds.

What I did feel, was that my soul had been strained through muslin and distilled into vapor, and all I could sense of myself now, was pure energy. *I-I must be dying then.* A chilling terror slowly began to besiege my mind. Even so, I sensed that it was accompanied by only the shadows of Fear's physical manifestations, which when I could not feel my heart racing on adrenaline, couldn't even close my eyes to the scene below, my whole reality became a deep dark well from which was building an ancient and unutterable scream.

Along with the dread, fueling its fire, was coming a strong deep love for this body below. I wanted nothing more than to be back down there, back inside my skin. I began to panic, sought to claw my way back down through the air. Thinking that maybe I could dive in through my ear, or bellybutton, I tried to get my arms to work. They felt as if strapped to my sides, or not there at all.

But apparently just wishing it was enough. Sinking slowly toward the little boat, I sensed a slight tugging from an elastic blur of silver energy, stretched between my floating consciousness and my seemingly lifeless body.

I kept sensing another energetic presence nearby, like the sense of being stared at from behind. My thought patterns began to oscillate through the oddest blend of warps and spastic jumps. Visions, memories, and dreams flashed in and out of my mind, threatening to overload my limited consciousness.

The boat lurched to one side as a last white-capped wave rolled in from the retreating tide. I watched my limp body roll face down in the grimy wooden hull. To my relief, I found that I could rotate my focus away for the moment, let something else attract my attention.

I was trying to calm myself as I slowly descended, by focusing on the images around me, and giving my imagination a bit of free rein. Down the beach to the west, the trio of seabirds, an ordinary family of gulls, was made suddenly extraordinary being the first birds from our world to come to the shores of this new place. Seemingly unbewildered at having found an island in their flight path, the birds tipped their wings into the brisk breezes and played their game of hopscotch down the strand past the whale remains, in search of a little luck, and then a likely spot to spend the night.

A kilometer to the west, the beach became rocky where the island rose more sharply up from the salty waters. Another kilometer, and there was no beach at all where the island met the sea at an almost right angle. The red cliff rose higher and higher as the western coast curved further out to the north.

Surely this wasn't the first time a soul had to come back from on its way to whatever awaits us after death, to find a way back into its cage. *Closer . . .* I slowly continued to spin until I was facing a dark stone giant.

From above I hadn't been able to tell what it was, but the huge stones of the point had been piled up and cleverly balanced to resemble a man, facing the sea. The sky was suddenly lit by a series of lightning flashes that gave the titanic statue the illusion of movement. A single long piece of shale took the form of an outstretched arm, pointing west.

Almost there now.

I was ready to beg for entrance to my own body, but I felt a definite smoothing shift in my perceptions as my consciousness easily reentered, *home.* There was an almost comical click, a physical wave of relief mixed with various aches, then darkness.

Girls' summer camp, and I had the luxury of one of the little canoes all to myself. Camp owned a large land tract where the Nigger Brown Creek met the upper northeast branch of the Altalanta. Despite the creek's regrettable name, I liked it for its deep narrow languid channel beneath the alders and willows.

My favorite thing to do at camp so far had been my own special brand of cloud gazing. I'd paddle up to about where the creek quickened, and turn the canoe around. Let the serene currents carry me back down the kilometer stretch, while I lay on my back on a blanket in the bottom.

Watching the sky, the clouds and branches sliding by overhead, gave me such a feeling of freedom in my heart, it would carry all my thoughts away–thoughts of life at home, of Mom, and of 'Darrell Dee; the-real-deal'. *What a jerk!*

It wasn't often that the other girls came this way. *They's no bus to haul your butt, and no trailer to haul your canoe.* This lent me a sense of solitude that I almost felt guilty over. *Why ain't I more like the other girls?* I crossed my arms under my head. I could be if I tried. Could at least look the part.

Above the arching alders, a particularly large dark cloud was rolling across the sun. I was happy for the shade it gave–this was my second trip and the morning was warming.

The cloud was slowly changing form as it lolled on. The canoe scraped the root of a submerged log, sending a shiver up my spine.

I came to the one long straight stretch where there were no overhanging branches. I was coming to feel the familiar sense of weightlessness that made the canoe disappear beneath me. We were traveling in the same general direction, the cloud and I. It was halfway across the sun when it took the shape of an immense floating bear.

We were flying through an eternal sky. I watched curiously as the huge bear slowly turned, as if to face me. As it turned, churning and billowing, it stretched its limbs outward. The whole cloud was expanding, causing the illusion that it was coming closer, and its back legs reached down to meld with another cloud below it, as if it were trying to stand.

The bear-cloud seemed to lean forward, and as it opened its mighty jaws, I had to remind myself, *it's only a cloud.* I'd almost, for a few seconds, been expecting a deafening roar to come out of those jaws. As it was, the sun was now pouring out of them, in brilliant silver rays, like the eye of God.

I was about to bring my arm up to block the light, when a sharp tug on the side of the canoe brought me completely back out of the clouds. Immediately, another stronger tug downward threatened to capsize me. Two sets of furred black claws curled over the top edge of the aluminum trim. A splash of water drenched my mid-section. A deep snorted grunt came from over the edge and sent a wave of panic through me as another vicious pull rocked the narrow craft.

I rolled with the canoe, and would've broken my nose on one of its ribs if I hadn't already had my arm halfway up to shade my eyes. I had only a split second to glance up at whatever was trying to tip the canoe. Its hairy jaws split in a wide sharp-toothed grin under deep-set green eyes.

It roared as it dipped its clumsy head in toward me!

The canoe started to bob, causing the strange animal to lose its grip. The side of the canoe came up and struck the underside of its jaw with bone wrenching force. I heard a cry and a splash, and—

A dream! . . . No. That really happened. Six years ago? Seven. I opened my eyes to blackness, closed them again. They hurt. My cheek was pressed into something wet and wooden. I couldn't move at first. The way I felt made me want to sink back into delirium.

I was finally able to get my left arm to move enough to put my gloved hand up under my head as a pillow. I rolled onto my left side, slowly–painfully. I saw a quick succession of bright flashes behind my eyelids and thought there was something really wrong with my brain, but some seconds later came the telling crack-boom-rumble of thunder. The murmurous rolling in and out of the waves was drawing me back under.

I brought my knees to my chest, tucked my right hand in my thighs–it was the only defense I could muster against the bone deep chill, before darkness again settled mercifully over me.

Third times' charm Willow–last chance now girl. It was mama's voice, or perhaps my own. I woke slowly to the sound of waves, odd visions clearing away in the dark. I opened my eyes to a blurry, floor level vantage point. With night having settled in, there wasn't much to see; dark wooden planks stained with splotches of something blackish.

The cold-blooded painful reality of my situation was slowly sinking in.

I must have slid my left glove off in my sleep, and my hand was cupped protectively over the back of my head under my hood. It took a bit of effort but I pulled my stiff left arm out from under me enough to get my upper body onto my elbows. An empty canteen rolled away.

My biggest concern when I first found myself stranded in the small boat on the strange island was the goose-egg at the base of my skull–and the fact that I couldn't remember how it got there. I could feel the sticky mess of dried and matted blood that clung to my hair. The pain at the site of the wound was itchy and intense, while the pain beneath it filled my head with an ache like kidney stones on the brain.

My next concern was the grinding empty pang of my belly. *Must've been in this boat a long time.* The wetness in my pants attested to this as much as the dryness in my throat.

Wonder what woke me, the growling coming from my belly, the pain banging around in my head, or my own stench?

Most of the angry clouds had disappeared to the south, and a three quarter moon was high on the rise. I turned my head, painfully, to survey the situation. Dimly I began to remember acquiring the old boat from the abandoned cottage up the Hexarkana. I saw my pack, precariously perched on the boat's back seat, saw the scattered .38-caliber rounds from one end of the boat to the other, and in the midst of them, one pistol, half submerged in water.

Shadows swam in the dark before my eyes as I lurched up onto my hands and knees. I'd formed a simple plan–*get up and get out of the boat fool, or else lay here and die*. I had never felt so weak, but I'd never been one to deny a matter of fact, or to turn down a challenge.

I crawled to get over the edge. I could make a successful effort at standing with my feet on the ground. The boat rolled back toward the sea when I took my arm off it. I was glad to see that it wasn't going anywhere. If I'd had to make a grab for it, I might have had to let it float away. As soon as I could, I would pull it farther onto land.

For the moment, I'd be better off on my knees, using the side of the boat for support. I edged sideways out to the back of my little ark, feeling worse than ever, nauseated and quaking with cold, a cocktail of aches rattling around my head. As the faculty of memory struggled to reestablish itself, I had to suppress the nagging question of whether the will to survive was equal to my present agony, especially in the light of the last few years. It would've been just as easy to reach for the pistol as the pack; *end it now, or prolong the misery?*

I'm not ashamed to say that I knelt there and peed my pants. I'd already done that and worse anyway, in my coma.

I kept pumping my fists until my arms were finally awake. I took the glove off my right hand, and pulled the other back onto the frozen left. My right hand trembled, but worked enough to fumble the clasp open on my pack. If memory served, Life itself, in the form of candy bars and an extra canteen was within reach.

I pawed the flap out of the way and started raking through the neatly stowed supplies, not caring that half of it was spilling out onto the damp floor.

I sat there leaning into the boat for a few minutes letting the water and sweet chocolate soak into my system. With my elbows resting on the boat and my head in my hands, I wasn't yet letting myself hope for too much. After a few minutes, I took three aspirin. Then for good measure, swallowed another.

I was still chilled through to the very bone, but realized that the air was only cool, not frigid. It's just that I was damp from urine and sea spray, from stem to stern. At least my pack was waterproof. One of my totes was strapped to a plastic sled in the back of the boat. I just couldn't remember how it got there, or why it would be flipped upside down.

I started to gather enough reason, and energy, to re-pack a few of the items I'd strewn. I also retrieved the empty .38 and soon had it resting on the back seat, reloaded with dry rounds. Lightning flashed, and the echoing of gunshots came from the depths of my mind, in time with the crackling thunder.

I looked up from the boat, away from the water—finally able to turn my attention to my surroundings. Everything was just as it had been in my unconscious visions—the electric silver moon, the stack-stone giant, the dark distant cone of an old volcano. *So where'm I?*

Worry about it in the morning. I groped down to check under the tarp—it was neatly secured over a nice little pile of split hardwood, and I recalled clearly, stacking the firewood there in the back, and covering it exactly as it was now. *What came after that? I think . . . No, I know.* I had then pushed the boat into the cold currents of ol' Narcsip'. By then I'd become good with the craft and had no trouble avoiding the more formidable ice floes.

With these clear memories came a sense of relief that my brain—indeed my whole sense of identity—was intact, at least for the moment.

I began shaking convulsively with cold and adrenalin. Since I'd so far found my body in unbroken condition from the neck down, I leaned into the boat and stood. Getting my sense of balance back, I began to jog in place to get my blood flowing. I was sure I'd have made a pathetic sight–also sure there was no one to see me.

It was just a feeling, possibly nurtured on the solitude I'd grown accustomed to, but I had never before felt so alone. The island's only other inhabitant was the great stone sentinel–the Rock God.

I took up a small armload of firewood from under the tarp, and soon had transferred several loads of the cordwood to a cluster of huge black boulders several dozen paces inland. That brought my temperature up enough to worry about other uncomfortable things.

I stripped the soiled clothes off the bottom half of my body and stashed the .38 in my coat pocket. The sea had finally sent its waves to rest. Without double-checking to see if anyone was around, I waded out into the chilly waters. A towel and my only dry pants hung folded over the side of the rowboat. The moon's reflection broke away from me in dozens of long brilliant crescents as my legs slowly disappeared.

I went out no further than I had to. The water wasn't as cold as I'd feared, or else I was colder. I worked my shirt and jacket up under my armpits, careful not to dump the pistol, and squatted in the water to wash up. I was almost finished when a sudden shudder of the ground beneath me put me off balance. I quickly changed my position to a tiger crouch to keep from falling over into the water face first. Another tremor followed–the boat tilted slightly back and forth as I watched.

By the time I pulled the fuse on the mini-thermite, I knew the meaning of the old phrase 'my goosebumps got goosebumps'. Shaking with bone-deep cold, I tossed the sparkling hissing tablet into the pyramid of waiting wood. The fire flared and crackled away in a matter of minutes. I felt a momentary flush of shame as I recalled Tuva's admonition to some of the guys at Fort Clifford, "No good spirits visit the fireside lit with gasoline." *Just this once old friend?* The wind lifted growing tongues of flames in a blue-green-gold vortex that danced and bowed.

I wrapped myself up in my one dry blanket and folded the tarp about me. In the seclusion afforded by the jumble of giant stones, I was soon warm and dry, if not cozy.

A great crashing noise shook me awake in the night, just as the moon was about to disappear over the horizon. Echoes of the sounds flew away on the sea breezes. The strange surroundings gave me a moment of terror, and I leaped to a shaky crouch, my old snub-nose drawn and cocked.

Tremors in the ground were fading away. To my left was the heaped ruin of rocks where hours before, the giant stone sentinel had stood.

I poked at the fire's remaining embers, threw on a couple small chunks of wood, and settled back into my nest to wait for the coming sunrise. When it finally dawned, still characteristically crimson from stratospheric dust, it was noticeably brighter than what I had become accustomed to since the catastrophe of last fall.

Over the next week I recovered, and watched in daily disbelief as beneath my feet, the island rose, slowly but surely, up and up from the depths of the ocean, coming up for air like some gigantic primordial sea turtle. The beach where I'd landed a high dune, and the western cliffs became a four hundred-meter sheer drop to the sea.

I wandered around a bit at the outskirts of the island, cautious out of old habit, and always on the move. All the gear and supplies I'd stowed on the rowboat, in several plastic totes, were in good shape. Of course, the outboard would never run again. If I had to stay here, at least I had all the comforts of camp.

Tremors gently rocked the island daily. The tops of palms and other trees would appear out in the surf in the morning; by night, a waterlogged forest had climbed up out of the waves. There were outcropping rocks in places where I could cup an ear to the cold stone to hear the deep grumbling, and mournful song, of the shifting aerth below.

There were actually two islands at the start. I had beached between a pair of dead volcanoes. A long bridge of land eventually emerged between them as the soggy ground arose from the sea.

I walked the circumference of the western island in a single strenuous excursion on my fourth day here, before the two became joined. After that, it became impossible. Every day, the island's acreage would increase exponentially. By the end of the first week, the total amount of land that I couldn't explore on my daily wanderings doubled. By then I'd started a map on one of the tablets of paper stashed in a tote under the overturned boat.

I saw no sense in trying to map the ever-changing and expanding shoreline, so I started with the part of the island that made up what I called 'the spine'. It stretched away from either end of the tombolo to link the two highest points, the jagged rims of the worn volcanoes. It would take weeks at the rate I was going to get to the east end.

In a small dense wood, was a flowing crystal spring, home to tiny white shrimp, between two of the formidable ridges that made up much of the island topography. The water I tasted there, gurgling up from under algae-draped rocks and huge old roots, was so sweet and clear that I decided to scout around for the best campsite within a few minutes' walk.

Making ever larger circles, with no small amount of effort, I found a spot up the side of one of the long forested ridges. A natural stone stair led up to a narrow but protected ledge half way up the slope. The 'perch' was some seven paces long and three to four paces wide–just enough room for my tent, a tarped-over table and chair, and a cookfire. Someone had made camp there before, though the evidence was not recent. I found ashes and cracked bones at about a hand-span down when digging out the most obvious spot for a small fire pit.

This seemed to be one of the wildest spots on the island, and as far as I was concerned, that was fine. A small clearing where several huge old trees had come down, between my new camp and the spring, became an excellent spot for a garden.

There were other signs around of a bygone civilization–I came across something new, and usually puzzling, every day. There were trails and stone roads, sprawling old orchards, circles of standing stones, and the occasional earthwork. There was also a remarkable trio of tall polished red-stone spires far to the east. As I discovered them, I would map and sketch them.

"I began to see more animals and their young."

My dwindling food supply was causing me worry.

Prior to my unaccountable arrival here, I had been on the lookout for any kind of packaged or portable edibles. With the constant cold on the mainland, refrigeration hadn't been a concern. And it had been easy enough to keep myself fed well, as long as I could thaw out whatever I found. After I'd commandeered the rowboat, I had even been able to accumulate a tote full of good food.

Most of the food I'd found here, was limited to some wild greens, and a few less than ripe carcasses which occasionally washed up on the beach. If I'd realized then, how many of the wild flowers are edible, I wouldn't have worried quite as much, because the island was becoming a painter's pallet of brilliant colors by the end of my first month as a castaway.

That was also about the time I saw the first animals. I was returning to my camp when a small speckled flightless bird with an audacious four-feather plume atop its tiny head, came bounding out of some bushes, as if it were spooked. It passed so near, I could have put my foot out to stop it, but it didn't seem to see me.

Without a sound, it disappeared like a bouncing ball into some undergrowth down the ridge. I stood there unable to move or even think for a short time. A single downy feather drifted overhead on a gentle wind, was carried up in a slow spiral, and away through the palm fronds.

A few seconds later, I was again surprised as a large grey lizard broke from the bushes on the trail of the funny little bird. It managed to look both ponderous and fierce at the same time. I'd been caught off guard, after a month of the island's isolation. The three wild shots I took at the advancing creature emphasized my lack of preparation, when all missed.

It too passed, seemingly unaware of my presence, focused only on the little bird it chased.

Unless I'm going deaf, they's something wrong here. Y'all didn't make a sound. Heard the shots though. I snapped my fingers and heard it clearly.

A short investigation uphill led me to the newly built nest, with a pair of speckled eggs that lured my hand like candy, but I resisted. Over the next few hungry weeks, I found more nests of various kinds, when I couldn't always resist.

The spring overflowed its rocky basin, spilled down a bank and away through the forest like quicksilver over a series of falls. The little creek also fed several small ponds as it wound its way south to the sea. Its waters finally became warm only where they mingled with those of the ocean, in the salty tidal pools of the southwestern lagoon. There I would periodically strip off my clothes during a hunt, for a quick dip.

I often wished I could bring myself to cast off reality along with my cutoffs and weapons on the soft sand, just at the edge of the gentle ripples. I eased cautiously into the tepid waters, only enough to clean up.

It had eventually dawned on me that I had to be prepared for just about anything. I'd seen enough animals, on wildlife shows and in my own travels through the real wild, to envy their instinctual alertness.

I need to become one of them. What is a human anyway, but another animal? We all have our gifts–and our limitations. We all have our separate roles in nature, and we all have the one big goal in common–to exist.

These thoughts, and being in the tidal pool, brought back memories of childhood fancies of being a mermaid. Thoughts of mermaids brought back memories more recent. Sometimes they would surface unexpectedly–disjointed visions of a long journey over water.

Also, I had begun to see more and more animals and their young. Some of the animals were of species familiar to me, but diminished in stature. Island life puts limits to growth on many of its residents. There were a number of species I didn't recognize at all, some that looked rather dangerous, and at least one oddball bird, that I knew from high school history classes to be extinct. I lost count of the different species at around a hundred.

I'd begun the practice of letting my instincts guide me. I cultivated a continuous wariness, and focused on honing and using all my senses, as well as my intuition. I even slept lighter, and with one hand curled around the lethal .38 caliber. I would have brought it into the pool with me, if it were waterproof.

I was about to finish when two nearly naked children bounded down the path. I'd only closed my eyes for a few heartbeats. Several paces from the water, the older girl–about eleven or twelve–stopped the younger with a hand on her shoulder. They hadn't made a sound, and I'd only enough time to dunk a bit lower into the water. I overcame my surprise but couldn't think of what to say. They had apparently come to swim.

They looked at me as if they were looking beyond me. I didn't know what *they* were sensing, but I was fairly sure that I was seeing two 'backwards' ghosts–they were like the animal apparitions. Indeed, they left no tracks to follow them by when they fled back up the path. But, in a week or so, these thin as air children would be as real to the touch as was I.

One morning I realized that the wretched nightmares I'd been plagued with over the last few years had stopped. I had to relish this with some amazement and much relief–couldn't remember when exactly, but knew I hadn't had one in *maybe* a month. I'd gone a week before, at most. I didn't dwell on it much though. This place had given me more than enough other things to ponder.

At least I didn't have to assume where I was. The remains of good old Americo were just over the horizon to the north. Trash with 'Made in Xiana' stamped on the bottom, washed ashore here every day. It was being flooded out of a hundred-thousand backyard dumps in the *big river's* vast watershed, and carried out to sea in great colorful flows.

The mainland's nine-month long winter had finally had its back broken by a month of continual coast-to-coast downpours. Now though it was August, and assuming a return to Aerda's natural cycle, winter would soon again be upon the northern continent. I sensed that the island somehow seemed to miss the worst of the weather.

The plants had originally suffered with the diminished light, nevertheless, the sky was clear enough now, and I had a good garden going. The seeds I'd planted were a motley variety–anything worth scavenging on my long trek south across the frozen former country of my birth.

What would I say to the islanders when we met, was a question I turned into a hundred different scenarios in my mind. It was wishful thinking. I hadn't seen the two children again, or anyone else, and maybe I never would.

Three months into my life as a castaway, the island stopped its slow upheaval. The last of the ground tremors faded away, by then I hardly noticed them anymore anyway. By my best estimations, there was now as much as one hundred fifty-square kilometers of land, and a couple hundred kilometers of coastline.

The two old volcanoes dominated the landscape at their respective poles to either end of the long low tombolo. I lived near the younger, but wasn't concerned much with the possibility of an eruption. Even all through the months of little earthquakes, as the island was being reborn, there was never any obvious venting of ash, or even steam.

My only explanation for the whole phenomenon of the island rising up out of the sea–after I'd had a chance to think about it–was that the ferocious gravitational pull of comet El Vaca coming so close to us, must have had a distorting effect on the planet's flexible mantle, especially near old volcanic hot spots between the cratons. The island had sunk in a cataclysm that had probably completely submerged all but maybe the tips of the volcanoes.

Then, the island would have been pushed back up by the compensating force of the planet's own overruling gravity, as its inherent elasticity on a global scale had once again brought the planet back into the shape of an almost perfect sphere.

That still left the unanswered question of the island's ghosts. *Was I hallucinating somehow?* And before that, the purging green flames that swept a whole country of people away like motes of dust. *And how are they all connected?*

Several otherwise unrelated sources had pointed to the end of the twelfth year of the twenty-second century as the end of 'a great cycle', a sort of harmonic celestial convergence. These prophesies, carried weight because they all came to a head simultaneously.

Different researchers, working separately, had kept hammering the same rusty old nail. Terra Schmeckle for instance; using computers, fractal mathematics and the Xianese U-Chung oracle system, the admittedly esoteric scholar noticed important waves of divisions throughout Aerda's long history.

According to Schmeckle, the last cycle began with the culmination of the Mad Hatter Project. This forty-eight-year cycle, at or near the end of a larger forty-eight-hundred year cycle, would terminate on December 21, 2112, midnight–exactly at the end of both the My'an and the Celto/Druidian calendars.

This was all useless information to most people though, for whatever reason. Most could repeat some of the facts and the theories associated with this particular end of the world scenario. But that was almost a year ago, and as near as I could figure, the end of the world came right on time.

I looked about, scanning the trees and bushes for anything out of the ordinary, trying to look unconcerned. I'd been on my way down to the clearing to harvest breakfast. Laid out at the bottom of the path on a wicker mat, was an odd surprise.

Atop a stack of three strange boxes was a narrow black case, the length of my forearm, which lay open to reveal a translucent rod. I reached out to the glass rod. Instead of picking it up, I nudged it with the backs of my knuckles. There was something between a tingle and a vibration.

I stooped to sniff the pile of items–nothing sinister, not that I could detect.

Gifts?

In the first of the large boxes was a new pillow, and new linens, and a self-inflating mattress that turned out to be quite comfortable over my old sleeping mat. The second big box was actually a self-chilling cooler, solar powered, full of foods of all kinds. The third was a chest of, among other things, handmade clothing, tailored to my size.

Over the course of the next few days I reveled in the exotic foods, and the luxury of new clothes. Through trial and error I figured out the workings of most of the more technical doodads. But I wondered who had left the packages, and why.

I awoke in the still dark from another of the 'city of gold' dreams. Wide-awake with wonder, I climbed outside to pee. The night was only half over.

In the time it had taken me to relieve myself, I saw that I was done with my period, and I had planned a long trip to the far end of the joined islands. I would trek down to the tombolo. If I couldn't make it quite that far by nightfall, I'd stay at my first campsite, the grave of the fallen Rock God. The old boat was still there, upside down on the boulders.

The islander's little lamps were quite handy in my preparations. I wanted to keep my pack less than forty kilos, which was easy enough by substituting with some of my newly acquired marvels.

Either of my old lamps, both state-of-the-art at any of the sporting goods stores of a year ago, weighed about a kilo and a half. I was already a good way into the charge on my last battery for one, and I had about a half liter of gas left for the other. Careful rationing would stretch the life of these two lamps only so far.

But the new lamps, looking for-all-the-world like Ping-Pong balls, weighed less than thirty grams each. They seemed to have no means of charging, no fuel port, and no battery slot–they had no seams or even switches. And they stuck wherever you put them, as long as you held them there for a few seconds (even in midair, but only for a few hours at a time).

A quick gentle double tap of one finger would turn them on or off. A series of taps with two fingers would cause them to brighten, and a series with one finger made them dim. Another function, which adjusted the type of wave length, and which filters it employed, was controlled by tracing left or right helical patterns on the lamp's surface. I'd found I could slide my fingers over the surface of the little globes in a certain way to concentrate the light so it shown out of only part of the sphere, even down to the size and intensity of a minor laser.

I learned all this from the lamps themselves–they seemed to have some internal programs and sensors that told them if someone who had no idea of what they were doing was handling them. An animated three-dimensional illustration had flickered to life in the air above the ball, and demonstrated the proper techniques to get the desired light. It used a number of intuitive sounds–whistles, clucks, and buzzes–in its training.

The translucent rod had a similar tutorial style of instructing a new user. It was a weapon, of sorts–a rather sophisticated and powerful one, but safer than any gun since it could never shoot-to-kill a human.

I guessed that it was an incredibly advanced technology, not magic, that made these things work. When I had held the rod up to the sky and looked at it from a certain angle, I could see its delicate inner workings, which I understood to be the crystal equivalent of transistors and circuit boards and a power system. *Maybe the science is in the magic, and the magic is in the science.*

I decided to lash the hatchet onto the pack frame. I saved space by taking a small tarp and a bit of rope instead of the tent–I could cut poles from sticks as needed–crammed in a few more things, packed a couple days worth of food on top, and clasped the flap shut. I strapped my skinning knife on–the .38 as well.

A two-minute sweep-through to tidy up camp gave me a last chance to keep from forgetting anything. There was no moon and I wanted to make good time, so I stuck one of the ping-pong lamps to the bill of my cap, and set it to searchlight mode.

Numerous traces of past human habitation existed all over the island, mostly ancient sturdy structures of stone. I'd noted on my map that they grew grander and more frequent, and newer, as I explored further from west to east.

Finally, I was going to meet them, the builders of the megaliths, and wondered as I walked, what had taken me so long.

AERDA AND ADERA

I saw them just as they saw me. I was two thirds of the way across the distance from my end of the island to the other, early on the second afternoon of my eastward journey, when I saw a few people in the shade of the landmark which I called the tri-obelisk, an ominous two-hundred-meter tall grouping of three red-stone spires. I had been beyond this place only twice, and not very far at that.

I maintained my composure–after all, I had not been skulking about as usual. They all turned their attentions my way. We waved a friendly greeting back and forth. It was all I could do, on one hand, to keep from running away, and on the other, to keep from running up to them and embracing them in my joy.

They were all short, of medium build and skin tone. They wore clothes of a style similar to the ones I'd been given the week before–sort of an 'Amish practicality meets the immortals of Zardoz look'. All had similar facial features, wide cheeks, hawkish noses, ears on the small side, cleft chins and mouths that looked made for singing. Finally, they all had sharp but honest eyes, the color of roasted chestnuts.

The women's thick coal black hair was as straight as mine was kinky–his was windblown, the color of straw.

The smaller woman, who had the merest hint of grey in her hair, appeared to want to speak for the group, and seemed to be trying to organize some means of communication. She held out her hand to the man, who handed her a small slender black rod. The other woman was meanwhile taking off a jeweled silver ring that she handed to me with an air of confidentiality.

The older woman whispered to the dark metal wand-like item. It beeped twice. She ran her fingers over its surface in a Pan-like dance, whispered again and touched her ring to its tip. Their language was as foreign to me as was their technology, but I soon learned that the former was a simple problem to overcome with the latter.

With the ring on my finger, and by directing my speech through it and having it analyzed by whatever programs operated the small cigar shaped device–which the older woman held at an arm's length between us–we talked. It took a few minutes of trial and error for the machine to make the link between our two languages, and bridge the centuries since the one had been spoken on Aerda.

"My name is Runa," she said. "We are from—" There were some words I didn't understand. She was pointing to the eastern caldera. "It is called Harth."

This was going to take a little getting used to. I could hear the words she spoke in her own language, muted compared to the words that seemed to form in the air above the cigar device. I immediately noticed the way the translator was able to reproduce the sound of her voice, better than her accent. It was the same when I spoke.

"Most people call me Willow," I said. "That is, they used to before. Been almost a year since I've actually talked with anyone, else." I hadn't meant to add the 'else', it just slipped out. If they took it to mean that I'd begun talking to myself . . . *So what.*

She gestured to the younger woman. "This is Jahna."

"Nice to meet you," I said and extended my hand, which Jahna grasped readily.

Runa nodded and smiled. Then I heard my name in what she said to Jahna. The younger woman tried my name, questioningly, as she held my hand.

Runa repeated the introduction with the man, whose name was Xoqueicue. I was having a little trouble pronouncing it and it made him smile. His grip was as warm and strong as his smile was warm and reassuring. There was a tiny inexplicable tug in my heart as he repeated my name in a voice like a wind through the trees–*through the willows.* I smiled back.

"Just call him Cho for short," said Runa. "We do."

"So this is your island?" I caught myself being conscious of how I was speaking–having almost said ". . . y'alls' island?" I stifled a dozen other questions, and proceeded to tell them about waking up marooned on the dunes and finding a place to camp–my perch.

". . . at the mighty stone monument to check for any damage the tremors might have caused."

I thought about asking exactly where we were, since my maps didn't show an island of this shape or size in the vicinity of where I *thought* we should be–the Gulf of Kalexico. I thought of asking them about the way the animal life had seemed to phase into existence over the course of my second month here. I considered asking where they had been while their island home was rising up out of the sea. Settled on, "Who exactly are you people?"

"Our knowledge extends farther back than any other in Aerdan history—" she began. Jahna made a small hand gesture, and questioned Runa.

"Yes, *that we know of*," said Runa, nodding at Jahna. She continued, "but, for the last two millennia, our people have lived here, on this isolated island."

"How can that be?" I asked. "I've never heard anything about any place like this."

"Just beyond the whippoorwill?" She turned to look at me out of the corners of her eyes. "Does that old expression still live?"

I shook my head.

"Where the sea meets the fog?"

"I've heard that one but, excuse me if I use a new one–*does not compute*."

"Of course, of course." Runa smiled warmly. She motioned to some low stone steps. "Let's get comfortable here, for a few minutes. We'll talk, then we have a long walk ahead. You'll come to Harth with us I hope?"

We sat in the shade of the immense spires. I took it from the look in Runa's eyes that she wondered if the rigged-up translator was up to the job of making her explanations understandable. Eventually she forged ahead, "We are of a people who *see* things a little differently." She tried to smile but I could detect an apology in it. "We are one of the last of Aerda's lines of Far Seers."

I motioned for her to continue.

"The history of the ancient craft of the Far Seers tells how an early people, coming in tune with cosmic energies, traveled unimaginable distances, and gained command over fantastic alternate worlds, but that they were outdone by their own natures, their human weaknesses.

"The ancient line fractured, and the same scenario played out once more, new lines split off again and again.

Some were destroyed by inexplicable forces, some were destroyed from within by the same old weaknesses, some were destroyed by a growing mentality of superstition.

"Nevertheless, there were certain lines that hung on and even flourished when they expanded their focus and learned to assimilate the knowledge available in what they saw, just beyond the whippoorwill," she gestured expansively.

"Great and wise men, around the world, led a new brand of Far Seers to wield true power. Th—"

I interrupted her. I was having more than a little trouble keeping up. "You mean this world?" I pointed at the ground, "Aerda?"

Runa nodded.

"What kind of power could hide a whole island?!"

"Not hide exactly. We've been gone, one hundred generations. We have come back now, as was agreed."

"Agreed?"

"The spirit that animates the universe took us. We don't know why, and it actually happened over several decades, but we were led to—"

Xoqueicue leaned forward and said something to Runa. She nodded her agreement and handed him the little computer that translated for us. His smile was encouraging enough, but I could have sworn he winked at me, and I made up my mind, without really thinking, to do whatever he was about to suggest.

"This will all make a lot more sense in Harth," he said. "The city has a way of speaking for itself. We were just heading back. Come with us. Runa will welcome you to stay with her for a few days."

They'd already finished their work at the Tri-obelisk–which they called M'nala Salinas–when I had come out of the wilderness to meet them. They'd been at the mighty stone monument to check for any damage the tremors might have caused. There was none. They were returning to Harth as they had come, on foot, since they had yet to convert their air transport drive systems to Aerda's still fluctuating field of magnetism.

I would have been right behind them then, as I had already made up my mind to fully transect the joined islands from west to east. "Of course I'll come," I said, nodding with some exaggeration, trying to convey my enthusiasm with body language, not trusting the emotion to a translating machine. They all smiled warmly. "Goin' that way anyway," I added with a shrug, and drew a round of laughter.

We traveled together at a brisk pace, single file. The islanders–they called the island Adera, themselves Aderans–were in good shape, as was I. We made it to the lower reaches of the outer edge of the caldera before sunset. We had traveled through diverse country, much the same as what I was accustomed to on the other side of the tombolo.

We were in a terraced clearing at the bottom of a wide trail. Several people worked the ground in fertile plots along both sides, taking advantage of the evening cool. The last light of the day was being slowly chased up the flank of the old volcano by Aerda's own shadow as the sun went down.

The path became a series of wide stone stairways. The steps appeared to be carved into the volcanic rock, although I was told that they were 'grown' out of the ground in the same manner as many of the other stone structures I'd mapped. Runa explained that they sculpted them with intricate applications of specially bred super-lichens.

There were overhanging terraces here and there up the slope to either side of the stairways. Some of the terraces held works of sculpted stone–from the elegantly simple, to the classically stately, to the otherworldly weird.

As we advanced, a flash of strange greenish light made a glorious spectacle on the land that rose so sharply before us. It illuminated the way the Aderans had sewn their art into the landscape, and into their lives.

"I was hoping to get here in time for you to see this," Runa spoke through the comring, smiling at me, again with that hint of an apology.

"It's glorious!" I said, looking up as the green light faded away quick as it had come.

"It will be dark by the time we reach the summit," she said. "You'll see Harth by its lights as we descend the stairs on the other side."

So far I hadn't seen any traces of gold, but I knew that in a sense, I'd come to the place my dreams had been trying to show me.

"We're tunneling through for one of our bullet trains here," said Runa. She pointed to a large flat circular stone foundation to the right side of the trail where the path turned to stairway. There were several large machines set up on the slab. "It should be done in ten days, from what I understand. There'll be a trade post built on that slab when the tunnel is finished. A five minute ride from there in the speed-chute and we'd be in the heart of the city."

"Well, who wouldn't prefer an hour of climbing, to a quick ride in a bullet?" I asked, letting my head loll to one side as I peered up at the imposing series of stairs.

Runa gave me a puzzled look, then she giggled. "I'm glad humor survived,"

I pulled the last carrot free from the black earth, knocked the loose dirt off, and nestled the root into a large sack. *Mammoth Copper Cores eh, they sure lived up to their name.* I had been a bit worried I was rushing them, but they looked good, and tasted great.

As we had arranged, Xoqueicue would be here soon. He could help with the rest of the harvest. He had said he was looking forward to it. The corns were next.

I was on my way down to the first of the little falls, to clean carrots, when the special comring they had assembled for me in Harth, buzzed on my finger. I un-slung the bag from my shoulder and sat it down as I stopped to catch the call. "Is that you Cho?" I asked after making the finger wiggling motion to open the channel for us.

"Yeah, it's me. Hi Willow." He was walking, by the sound of it. "How comes the harvest?"

"Good good. I'm just on my way down to the creek to wash carrots. I'll probably meet you on the way up. How was the sailing?"

"Oh, it was good. We'll have better winds on the way back."

Sensing there was something he wasn't saying, I paused.

"Willow, I was hoping to be to you by now, but . . . well—"

"You're lost, aren't you?"

"How'd you guess?"

"I know how men are with directions."

"Only when it's a woman giving them."

"Besides," I said, "you people already knew where I lived."

"That wasn't me, if you're talking about the care packages. Guess I could have asked Njafria for better directions."

I tried not to let the term 'care packages' sting too much. In English it carried connotations of charity. I wondered, could a translation machine be so sophisticated as to pick up such intricacies of thought. Besides, I hadn't seen any typical signs of charity, or even any need for it, during my short stay in Harth.

"You mean, better directions than turn left at the second big clump of palm trees?" I asked, garnering a laugh from him.

"As for better directions," I said, "I do remember specifically saying, to anchor in the little lagoon where the southwest cliffs part."

"Did that."

"And then to just follow the little creek, from the pools up to the spring."

"I thought I knew a shortcut."

"I don't think there is one . . ."

"I've got a plan," he said finally.

"Go ahead."

"When I tell you to, you've got to activate a signal on your comring to synchronize it with mine."

"Sounds exciting," I purred. *Oh—Oops. That was flirting. I hardly know the man. Maybe they don't know about flir—*

"You just press on the bottom of the ring with your thumb while you tap three times on the crystal. I'll hold the channel open while my ring locks onto your position."

"Whatever you say," I replied as I performed the little procedure.

I had the carrots rinsed and packed by the time Xoqueicue found me.

We spent most of the day silently harvesting the last of my summer's labors. He really seemed to enjoy the work, and my company.

We took my camp apart in a surprisingly short time, and I found myself saddened by it as I stood there looking back at the empty place of which I'd grown so fond.

"I've only been here a few hours," said Xoqueicue warmly, "but I feel like I'm going to miss it when we leave."

"Me too. I'll come back someday."

"I hope you'll bring me with you."

I smiled at him. *Maybe they do know how to flirt.*

"So, this place I'll be staying in Harth?"

"The dorm at Sky Garden—it's nice," he said. "I've been there. It's a school actually." 'Nice' turned out to be an understatement in the extreme, to me anyway. Sky Garden became my wings.

We had everything packed in boxes and arranged neatly on a thick plastic mat. I was ready to start lugging the first few items. The several trips would take us until after dark.

Xoqueicue touched my arm. He had a mischievous grin. "Watch," he said as he ran his fingers across a device on his wrist. To my astonishment, the entire mat full of my belongings rose with a hum, up to about a meter off the ground. He gave the load a push as he grabbed the rope that served as tether. "There's no propulsion system yet."

Xoqueicue and I came out to the library patio, each with a handful of maps and works on Aerda's history from the Far Seer's perspective.

As I learned the language, I also came to learn that the island city was one of several around the world whose inhabitants had practiced an esoteric art they called Far Sight. In effect, they had learned to dream so well that they had taken themselves out of this world, to wait, and to learn, and one day, to return.

I studied some of this in the lesson courses, afternoons at Sky Garden, and got some of it from Xoqueicue. He and Runa had each come to see me several times as I was getting settled in. The program that translated for us had gotten quite good at it over the weeks, but we all looked forward to the time when it wasn't needed.

They both wanted to take me through the 'city' too. Harth was more of a large sprawling village than any city.

There were more gardens than buildings and more trees than gardens, but who wants to argue with a talking machine.

The view from the veranda where I sat with Xoquei-cue was utterly enchanting. We were just outside the Sunrise Library on the little promontory above Circle Cove.

People strolled along on the path below. A group of older people came down the steps from the library. Several couples were already here when we arrived. The veranda was a popular place for its view. To the east was the tower called Lac Syph. It was carved from black granite and white quartz, inlaid with gold and mother-of-pearl. If M'nala Salinas could vie for the eighth wonder of the ancient world, and I believed it could, Lac Syph would have easily made number nine. Both were artifacts of great engineering and art, as well as age and power. This power was tied into the island, and had somehow helped to maintain it away from the bosom of Mother Aerda.

The tower sat up at the same lofty height as the library, where we were, and the girls' school to the west at Sky Garden, where I lived. Everything else but the sky was below. Outside the caldera was the wide glinting ocean, inside was Harth and the cove of gold and aquamarine.

Circle Cove had formed when wave action had, in ages past, carved one portion of the caldera away and let in the sea. It had flooded more than two square kilometers to a depth of about sixteen meters.

There were pathways and scooter trails, and little bullet trains, and sky wires, instead of roads. One wide avenue partially encircled Circle Cove, by way of the elegant suspension bridge over the narrow inlet. The avenue was used by a variety of electric trucks, hundreds of scooters, pedestrians, pedal bikes, and whatnot, but nothing to approximate the automobiles of my wild teen years.

I had been seeing the first experimental translifts too. They looked like a cross between a hovercraft and a minibus. There had been some horrendous accidents, and the project engineers were taking a whipping in the public's eye over too many deaths. Apparently, they would never function over deep water, but they were working on plans for submarine convertibles.

Near the center of the submerged area was a small green island–a much younger, much smaller cone, born inside the huge old crater. It too had sputtered and died in the far reaches of time before the first men made their own fires. The Aderans called the little cone shaped island, Birgea Il V'ansuriah, which meant 'last refuge of the first Far Seers'.

"That's from the old tongue," said Xoqueicue. "Only a few still know the language, but what the name refers to is the legend of Kuarok and Oau, the two from whence came the first of our kind."

"It's beautiful," I said. "Can we go there?"

"We can, but only in our dreaming. It's a preserve."

We began unpacking the contents of our baskets. Xoqueicue had brought puccics–fresh baked, still warm–I'd have called them bread sticks. I had brought a spicy sweet tomatillo sauce, which went well as a dip for the puccics.

The Aderans weren't ones to have prayer prior to eating, or prior to anything as a rule. Neither was I, having been ruined for that sort of thing as a girl. However, there was in their approach to everything, a sense of practical reverence. The act of taking a meal was itself a sort of prayer. We ate the puccics in silence, with an appreciation that made me realize I had finally learned to eat, at twenty-two.

Xoqueicue had the afternoon off from his duties out on the water. He performed maintenance on the various projects the islanders had going on in the extensive reef areas. His expertise was in engineering R'smar Kettma, the growing of stone into the structures the Aderans used. His love was for shallow diving. So, he worked on the wind derricks, and the underwater observatories and such. When I heard this, I thought about sharks, and worried for his welfare.

I poured us a couple of small cups of the Aderan's sinfully delicious wvintu to wash down the first course of our late lunch. Wvintu was about as strong as hard cider when its still fizzy–not something you could get drunk on, but it was a mood shifter. It was the only drink on the island with any alcohol at all, but without exception, it was used more for its healthful properties than for the buzz. If they wanted to get out of their heads, the Aderans had other ways.

"Never thought ah'd see so much beauty in one place," I said, looking out over the cove, and Harth.

I was sipping at my cup thinking about what a romantic moment this could be if only Xoqueicue would reply with something like, *I never thought I'd see so much beauty in one face.* Not that I thought he wanted anything more than my company, or that I was near pretty. *Goosey.* I had to keep from laughing at myself.

Xoqueicue pulled a small package out of his basket. "This should go good with the wvintu." And it actually did, to my surprise–it was smoked shark.

"Where'd you get it?"

"Killed it on my last trip out to the southernmost weather station."

"Maybe I should worry for the sharks."

He bared his teeth and we both laughed aloud.

We finished the salted meat and some of the fruit I had brought. I'd no sooner wiped my lips when Xoqueicue asked me to tell him everything I knew about dreams.

We were trying more and more to converse without the use of the comrings as translators, but I thought that dreaming was a subject that called for a deeper understanding, so I activated mine.

"What can you say about dreams? They are mysterious, elusive . . . powerful sometimes. A hundred different people will give you a hundred different estimations of what they're worth."

He *seemed* to be listening, waiting for more. I noted his gaze was often drawn to the ocean, especially if some of the islander's boats were at sea, or if, as was the case from here, the offshore windmills were in sight.

I continued. "Some people will tell you they don't dream, which really only means, they cain't remember 'em. Others will say they dream this way or that . . . never had anyone tell me they dream in black and white.

"Some say dreams are our deepest and truest wishes, but that they are veiled in random nerve impulses flooding up from the lower cerebral cortex, and that the resting brain just does its best to try to make sense of it all."

"You've done a bit of study–go on," he said.

"Yeah, well I don't know if I really learned anything important. Some of those dusty old books would have us believe dreams can be clarified, and measured, using symbolism that's common to dreamers. Used to be a lot of head doctors big on that whole thing.

"Other people flat out refuse to talk about the subject. Either they're too practical to be bothered with such—" I grasped for the right word–not sure I'd found it, I resumed, "*flack*, or their dreams are too personal to divulge to anyone else."

I wasn't sure of what else to say, and didn't mind leaving off on that note. *Maybe my own dreams are too personal to talk about.*

"But what do you know from your own experience?" He prodded. "Dreams need to be probed, played with, experimented with. You can't rely on someone else to do this for you."

"Right," I said. "You mean like sleep researchers, 'white coats' in laboratories, with people hooked to monitors all night. Hundreds of books have been written 'bout dreaming." I was actually only guessing at that number. "And, considering the pages on pages of contradictory material, I'd say the subject has been way overworked. Half of it must be dead wrong. I'd maybe even go so far as to call 90 percent of—"

He held up a hand to stop me, and smiled gently to reassure me, "I don't know about these laboratories in white coats, but I know there's no need for any machines. What I am concerned with is, how dreams relate to me, as I'm dreaming, *and* during my waking hours. Dreams are a highly personal experience for me. They have to be dealt with on a personal level. To know about dreams, you must know yourself."

"But, why bother? I mean, is it useful? People might think I'm strange."

Xoqueicue smiled. "I for one will consider you strange–that's a compliment. But, it can be a most worthwhile pursuit, and not a bother at all."

"You mean, beyond your own private entertainment, or the shrink's couch?"

Xoqueicue gave me a puzzling look. I took it to mean he was trying to follow me into my world.

"Let's say you have a vivid dream," he began, "and you remember it fully upon waking, so you write it down as sort of an outline, and then later you flesh in the details. Then you examine it from every angle as it relates to your life, and you make certain conclusions about why you had this dream. Being honest with yourself, and to your dream, may help solve some problem you're having." With a nod and a side-ways swipe of his hand, he communicated that this was all elementary.

I nodded in agreement.

He continued, "You've probably had a series of dreams, or nightmares, that seem to come in sequence and build upon each other, maybe not night after night, but often enough to make a connection. These are dreams to pay attention to. They are a definite signal to you. It *may* help to talk to someone about them, unless you are in tune with yourself and your surroundings. It is a great waste to just ignore such gifts.

"Now let me ask you this—how often in your daily affairs, while you are wide awake, do you say to yourself, 'This is a dream'?"

"Um . . . I, not very often, like never," but as soon as it had passed my lips, I remembered the 'city of gold' dreams, from a few months prior. "Well, to be truthful, I never would've, before coming here." I actually had to resist the momentary urge to pinch myself there and then.

"And you probably don't say it, or even think it, *while* you're dreaming do you? Yet, when you're standing naked in the town square, instead of laughing about the pre-posterousness of such a weird dream, you get embarrassed.

"Or, when you're sitting on the couch next to your lover, with your clothes peeling off like 'charuva' skins," he held up one of the little yellow fruits, which I would have called a banana, "your blood pumping hot through your veins, and . . ." He made a sort of finger spiraling gesture which I took to mean, 'one thing leads to another', "Do you take a deep breath and, do you ask yourself, 'who is this amorous so and so, and what am I doing here?' Most people wouldn't."

I mimicked his finger twirling. *Go on.*

"You are dreaming a good portion of your life away, and it seems so real and natural while its happening, you don't even stop to question it. So, do you make use of these altered realities, or do you forget them?" He seemed to think the answer was obvious.

I shrugged.

"Do you seek to explore the power of dreams, or do you embrace the waking world of the day, and your body's fight for supremacy over your spirit?"

"You're talking about lucid dreaming, aren't you?"

"Maybe. Explain."

"Lucid dreaming, supposedly, is a state of comprehension. It's said to be hard to achieve and even harder to maintain–practiced by few, and mastered only after years of effort."

He shook his head. "If lucid dreaming means, it's possible to attain control over your actions in dreaming. If it allows you to truly put dreams to use, to do what you want to, go where you want to, in worlds that are as real and significant as this one, then yes, I'm talking about lucid dreaming."

Giggles and chatter preceded a pair of young girls strolling along the path below the veranda. Our eyes met. We'd seen each other before. It was the two from a few months prior, at the tidal pools. They seemed to recognize me. I waved them over.

Xoqueicue welcomed them warmly. He knew them, and introduced us, "Alekis" he motioned to the younger, and then the older, "and Llikka. Biggest troublemakers on the island. Used to be anyway. Girls meet Willow–You've got competition now, I think."

We shook hands, and all made funny faces at Xoqueicue.

I asked the girls to sit with us, hoping to hear their version of the day they found me there bathing in the pool. Instead, I was asked one question after another about my arrival on Adera, and how I lived in the woods, and what was the rest of the world really like, until Xoqueicue finally interrupted them. He jogged their memories as to what they had been on their way to do. The girls' eyes got wide as they looked at each other. Without another word, they went squealing and flitting off like the first time I'd seen them.

"They're the ones who first mentioned they saw you."

"I wondered," I said.

That was about what our first 'date' amounted to. Hadn't expected kissing of course, but a part of me had missed it. He was so fine! *Will power Willow*. Sometimes I caught myself thinking in my mother's voice.

I thought I had developed an impeccable sense of discipline, until coming up against learning to dream. The training was practiced as an artist practices painting–arduously, but not as a practical means to a practical end. At first, I had to convince myself that it wasn't the Aderan's substitute for TV.

Over the seasons that followed until summer came again, I worked to gain the skills of the Far Seer's dreaming. But this technique didn't come for free. I had to cultivate it, like working the communal gardens. I had to court it, to really want it–like I told myself I wanted Xoqueicue. And I had to believe I could do it, practice during the night, and in my spare time during the day.

Laurentia. I could almost forget why we were here when I looked around at the beauty of the snow laden firs. Except for the occasional whistle of a slight breeze, and the accompanying muted plops of snow falling off the fir boughs, all was quiet when we were still, *at ease*, which wasn't often.

The hypnotic rhythm of the diagonal stride–the slice-slice of skis on snow–invited my mind to wander. Snowshoes were ok, but I had come to prefer the skis, and gotten pretty good with them too.

I was thinking of an old song by the Wee Peas when we came across the tracks. Tuva saw them before I did. Being the smart-ass he always was, he said, "Saw dem forty paces back, soon as we made the ridge there."

"That's your Eskimo eyes man," I said, baiting his temper with a little 'raw meat'.

He shook his head comically as he made a chalking-up motion. "Two points."

"How do your people flip the bird Tuva? Y'all could've just pointed 'em out when you saw them. I see they're old."

"Couple days."

I un-slung my rifle and leaned it against a tree. I had to pee–had for the last kilometer. I looked enviously at Tuva. Not for his built-in outdoor plumbing–*that shit comes with a permanent dose of testosterone, I'll squat*–I was envious of his ability to take the cold. He didn't need all the heavily in-sulated clothing. I was getting better though, with the tech-nique he'd shown me to accept the cold, like a brother, or in my case, a sister.

"Tuva, can you turn around or something, before I dance right out of these pants?"

"Sure," he said. "Think I'll just mosey this way a few. When you're done, you can cover me."

I guess the guy in the woods down the hill must have liked my backside, because the shooting didn't start until I had it covered back up.

The shots came regular and quick. *A practiced marksman!* I nose-dived for my rifle. If I'd stopped to fumble with the top two buttons of my pants, I'd be dead.

POP. POP.

Tuva dodged toward me. The shots came from be-hind him. They were striking the trunk of the small tree where I'd taken cover.

"Get behind here!" I yelled.

POP. POP.

I quickly planned a straight line route up the hill that would keep the protection of the tree I was leaving, between me and the shooter. There was only room for one of us there, so I lunged from the trunk, one hand holding up my pants, the other clasping the M-16. I headed for a huge fallen tree up the slope. It was the best place for a chance to turn this impending disaster around.

There was a pause in the shooting.

A few seconds after I hit the ground behind the great log, I heard Tuva make it to the tree below. I had to hand it to him–he didn't sound scared. I hoped he didn't have a reason to be.

"Cover me," he warned. He started to run as soon as I signaled him that I was ready.

He followed my tracks at a dead run, not something the Ivik-Tuvik should be especially good at with their com-pact frames, but snow was their element.

I saw the shooter as he left cover to take a few shots. I had a narrow band of un-obscured sight through the trees. I zeroed in and started a series that would begin at his neck, and end at his groin, in as short a time as I could squeeze off three triple-shots. TAT TAT TAT.

Tuva dived over the log a couple meters to my left. TAT TAT TAT. He did a neat somersault as I slung lead down the hillside.

TAT TAT TAT.

The shooter lurched once–took another wild shot–lurched twice, and sank back behind his tree.

"I think we got him," I said, containing my excitement.

Tuva was sprawled behind the log. His rifle lay beneath him at an odd angle that couldn't have been comfortable. His head was buried in the deep drift. The snow was starting to turn red. I plunged toward him in sudden horror.

I pushed his shoulder. "Tuva! EFFIN' HELL man! This is my-my fault–you can't!"

Slowly, he raised his head. My heart stopped. Bits of his brain lay glistening in the snow. For a split second, his face was gone. I turned away, purely from reflex. After a few deep breaths, I looked back, expecting again to see his head buried in the snow.

"I'm OK," he said. "How you doing?" There was a spot of blood over one thin eyebrow. I stared at him for a minute or so, slightly shaking my head in disbelief. The little circle of blood pulsed, and slowly closed.

I didn't have the heart to tell him, this was a dream.

I hardly slept the rest of the night.

As the sun was rising high over Sky Gardens, young Annrio came dashing into the garden, pretty as one of Aunt Sophie's peach blossoms. "Sorry I'm late Miss Willow," she gasped.

"Slow down girl. This isn't a landing pad," I said with a smile.

"I know I'm late if the sun is on the gate handle."

"I can see you feel bad about it. The best way to cure that is for us to get to work on those slugs."

"Ughs!"

"You gonna be late tomorrow?"

"Oh no."

"Good," I said. "'cause it's getting to be that time of year. Probably be just as many slugs tomorrow, and the world needs more like us to guard against the slimy little lettuce lovers."

"Right," she said, somewhat doubtfully, still catching her breath.

"So, why were you late?"

"Out last night." Her gaze dropped to the patch of ground between our bare feet.

"A guy?"

She laid her left hand across the top of her chest. "Uh, a slug." She put one finger up to her chin, gazed up at me questioningly, then smiled sardonically, and we both laughed.

Who's she remind me of when she smiles like that?

"After your lettuce then was he? I know the type." *I wish! How long has it been?*

"Kinda . . . You know," she said wistfully, "just because I was born a girl, I don't think that means I was made for a guy."

We went to the shed to get our gear. I didn't mean to let her last statement hang there in the air like that, but something about it was tugging at the bass strings of my memory.

My mind was so taken with trying to dredge up the particular memory that I absently brushed arms with Annrio in the confines of the tool corner. By her subtle reaction, I could tell that she welcomed the contact. By the tumbling feeling in my belly, I could tell that some part of me welcomed it too.

Suddenly it came to me—*Girl's Camp on the Altalanta!*

Megan! The canoe. Annrio looked and sounded like the junior counselor who had almost capsized me.

It had been intended as a practical joke, and to make it more effective, Megan had put on a rubber Halloween mask from the movie, Planet of the Apes. I'd secretly liked her up to that point. As for it being a joke, nobody was laughing—what with all the blood. For the first few minutes afterward, we were both holding our noses, thinking they were broken—It was only by dumb luck that they weren't.

Megan had been so apologetic—even through a wad of blood soaked tissues as we made our way to the nurse's office, even while the other girls tried to lighten the mood with good-natured jibs like, "y'all should Eskimo-kiss and be blood sisters," or, "how's boogery blood taste?"

Later that evening, she asked me to stay by the fire with her after the marshmallows were gone, and the others had told all the ghost stories they knew. We talked for an hour, about life and other mysteries, swatting the occasional mosquito, letting the fire die down on its own. I couldn't stay mad at her.

Then she came back to the 'incident in the creek'.

"I was dared to do it. Just bored I guess. Nobody was supposed to get hurt. Look. It don't mean they don't like you. Hell, I bet most of 'em go around thinking no one likes them, really."

"Don't care if they do or don't," I said.

"Well, it never hurts to have someone on your side," she said gently. "So much the better when that someone likes you."

It sounded wise, the way she put it, for a white chick anyway, and I nodded. We sat awhile in the warm red glow.

"You won't say anything, will you?"

I thought it a strange question, until I looked up to see that she was holding a lighter in one hand, and waggling a cigarette in the other.

"Oh! Well no." I smiled, and scooted a little closer to her. "In fact . . ."

She scooted even closer to me. We huddled and smoked, and after she tossed the butt onto the fire, her hand came slowly down on mine. When I didn't flinch, she said, "I guess I didn't want you to know," she hesitated, shuffling her feet, "that I like you the way I do, so I took the dare."

I became mesmerized watching the last wisps of our cigarette smoke above us, mingling with the smoke of the dying fire, and I felt as if my elated spirit was up there rising and swirling with the warm air.

"It was dumb, I know," she said. My gaze fell to the side of her pale delicate face as she continued. "Maybe I didn't want to admit it myself." Her piercing eyes–beautiful even in this light–turned to mine. "Do you think that just be-cause you're born a girl, it means you're made for a guy?"

Annrio looked up at me across the end of the bed of purple curled leaf lettuce. "Done," she said.

"Wasn't so bad was it?"

She shrugged. "What's next?"

"Wash your hands, we'll have some tea, and then thin the radishes in R-11 one last time."

While we were drinking our tea under the little arbor, I realized that something had changed about Annrio. Her eyes had turned blue–they were Megan's. My jaw dropped, but for only a split second.

A dream. Interesting. Glad I realized it before we went back to work. I spent enough time grubbing around in the dirt during the day, and more than enough time pulling my own reins–this, I was going to thoroughly enjoy. The tummy tumbling feeling came back, and a swirl of butterflies danced around us for a few seconds, on their way from the morning glories to the garden wall.

"Annrio, d'I ever show you, there's a bed in the back part of the shed that folds in and out from the wall. It's there for if anyone wants to catch a nap in the afternoon." I was just making this up, but I knew the bed would be there, while our dream lasted.

The dishes seemed to sing on the shelves of Xoquei-cue's kitchen with the intensity of our argument. "It was one sighting Willow! Calm down. The elde—"

"How can you tell me to calm down? They're COM-ING Cho," I ranted. "It's what they do! They'll come and take it all! What they don't take, they'll tear down–and they'll kill anyone who stands in their way!"

"It was just a ship on the horizon."

"There'll be more, and they'll bring war! Don't you get it dude?"

"It was weeks ago," he said.

"Look. I used to dream about this place. It was as if Harth was calling me. In my dreams, I saw her as a city of gold."

"Do you think the city is actually calling out to the rest of mankind?"

"I don't know! Doesn't matter!"

"Why not?"

"Because, they're the *don't call me, we'll find you* type," I said, shaking my head.

He spread his hands in acquiescence. "If it's gold they want, we'll just show them how to make all they can use, but—"

"They won't be satisfied with that. Cain't you under-stand, they've got their rules. You'd have to make it for them. I don't know what it was like before your people left the world, but there's something dark buried in the back of man's collective *whatever* that has to do this."

"The conquistador gene?"

"You know the word? What do you know of the conquistadors?"

"Only theory. We had ways of keeping informed about the plights of some of our fellow Far Seers. But it was extremely limited." He spread his hands out on the counter, looked to the dark corners of the ceiling, seemed about to go off to look for some book to reference his point.

"We'll never know what might have been if the Spaynish had never set foot on the shores of the 'new world'," I said. "It was one of our greatest losses. But it was just one, in a long chain of exterminations that fell across the face of . . . the whole world really. The Spayniards were just more *glorious* about it."

"I suppose if it hadn't been them, it would've been someone else," said Xoqueicue.

"Right. You people think you're safe, with your fan-cy technology, and your *magic*. So did the Axtec . . . the Ab-Originals . . . the Roamans, and so many others.

"The civilizations that existed in the Americos long before the coming of the Europans were in many ways supe-rior, except in their weapons of war." I slapped my hand on the table. "Nations of grand scale and wondrous accom-plishments, gone!"

"We don't believe that will happen here."

"You're naive. I'm sorry, but y'all got a bit out of touch after two thousand years in Whippoorwillville. The Conquistadors brought death with them, overwhelming greed, treachery, disease, lust–of course lust–cain't go any-where without that! With their guns and their swords they cut the brave Indyans down like stalks of wheat. Millions of people were overcome by mere hundreds! Huge cities, in-vaded and stripped in the Spayniard's consuming passion for gold and conquest."

I wondered how I could convince him that the rea-sons wouldn't matter. The new invaders would be the same as the old, and any reason would do. "Like I said, they'll do it just because that's what they do. Entire cultures were just wiped out. Others existed as mere shadows of their former glory."

In my mind's eye I was seeing all the weapons of mass destruction, still nestled in their silos. How long would it be before Aerda's scattered survivors figured out how to reboot those? *They'll nuke us out of spite.*

"That's the reality of it, on our world," said Xoqueicue. He reached over to the counter and picked up a round purple bulb, which he studied as he held it up between us. "But there are many other realities, like the skins of a nomyen plant, next to each other, but separate. And you can enter there if you try—"

We didn't seem to be hearing each other anymore.

"This is a dream. Isn't it?" I asked, even as I felt myself waking.

I loved the way the window was situated in my old place in the Sky Garden women's dorm. There, I could always rely on the sun to wake me if I slept late. The lives of the Aderans weren't ordered by hours and minutes, even so, everything seemed to happen when it needed to.

I was often amazed at how well they, *we*, all worked together. I had long been cultivating the penchant for rising early. Lacking an alarm clock–though I was sure we could have rigged up something in less time than it had taken Runa to assemble a translator–I was still somehow able to get everything done each day before the sun was midway across the sky.

Bet the sun's on the handle of the garden gate.

I sat up when Annrio knocked, told her I'd be right out, and sat for a moment on the edge of the bed relishing the fleeting memory of the dream of our lovemaking. I sensed a certain squishiness downstairs as I scooted to the edge of the bed. Part of me obviously wished it wasn't just a dream.

I was not feeling well rested. In my soul was a deep guilt over Tuva's death. In my mind was a growing anguish over the Aderan's self-isolation. And in my heart was a mix of emotions that seemed to overrule all else. The words of an old song by the Smiths slipped between the cracks of my conflicted feelings. *Last night I dreamed, somebody loved me.* I edged off the bed, into my slippers, humming the melody.

Me and Annrio? Hmm. I pulled on my gardening clothes. "No hope . . . no harm," I sang softly to myself, "just another false alarm." I put the song out of my head and opened the front door.

I spent the morning side by side with the young intern, working in the beds of lush green. Her eyes held a trace of Megan's ghost, and her laughter was water to a thirsty heart.

I was in a hurry to finish my gardening duties so we could meet as planned, when I got a call on my comring–I took it in my mind, and found Xoqueicue would be late. It was closer to sunset when we met.

Sometimes we got together at his place overlooking the north point–sometimes at my new place on the backside of the caldera, the western slope. I had moved there from the women's dorm, and into a triplex two thirds of the way up 'Vin Othe Goa', which was Aderan for 'the four-dozen and one stone stairways'. But this time, we met at our accustomed spot on the library veranda over Circle Cove.

I began to tell Xoqueicue of my dream about our argument, and how I was sure it was important. To my surprise, he did know about the Conquistadors–which precipitated another argument then and there–which felt like deja vu, but I knew somehow that it wasn't a dream this time.

We decided to drop it for the time being, and to resume the history lessons he'd been giving me.

Xoqueicue had an amazing memory for the history of his people. We had been going over it for a year in our infrequent meetings. I'd ceased thinking of them as dates long before–I still wondered if he ever had.

We'd covered over ten-thousand years of the Far Seer's history, and we were finally up to the point where this group of them went away to another reality.

"So, they were going through this major upheaval of thoughts and methods before the departure?" I asked.

I guessed I was about to get a short recap of a lot of stuff I already knew, which was fine. Most men I'd known, before, would go on and on about football or some other such nonsense.

"Nothing is ever as clear as we would like it to be," he said.

He led me through the extensive list of the Far Seer's major achievements and failures. They had spawned all the world's witch doctors and sorcerers, all the mystics and court magicians, alchemists and healers alike.

"When the old line first divided, only Kuarok and Oau carried the germ of true potential, true knowledge. Their line extends unbroken to this day, in us."

I was at once both flattered, and apprehensive, that he had included me in 'us'.

ART AND RELIGION

Dawn. Thirteen years later.

As an honorary elder of Harth–not that I was at all old, but at thirty-six, I was the oldest person from off the island–I was often called on to teach the children what I could, and happy to do it.

Actually, I was the only person from off the island, even after all these years.

For several years, I'd been gathering the kids on my walks through Harth, on days when the weather permitted, and taking them down the hillside to the Circle Cove beach, or sometimes to the southeast lagoon. I'd tell them stories and teach them mathematics or martial arts, and how to build fires and roast clams, or just swim.

This day, however, we had taken one of the new six-person translifts–*ten-person* if the persons be small–for the first leg of a much longer journey.

I brought the unit down in a clearing at a 'Y' in Adera's lengthy north trail. Our destination was a half-kilometer to the west, the new little village of Yaloway. The right-hand trail was more direct, and almost all downhill, but the left would take us along the ridge of the dunes, and by the remains of my old rowboat.

It was still quite early. As we walked by the lucky sight of my long-ago landing, I made sure that my entourage of little ones had plenty of time to stop and study the old rusty outboard.

I'd been back here myself quite a number of times over the years, so I was used to the way the Aderans had memorialized the sight with a little plaque, and a bit touched by it, to tell the truth. They had even preserved the boat so that the wood would never rot.

As the kids marveled over the few relics of a world they would never know, I was drawn inland a bit to the spot where I had spent that first night here. Out of respect, I resisted the old temptation to climb the jumble of rocks that had once stood tall, like a beacon on the sea.

I'd taken this decidedly indirect route, not just for nostalgia's sake, and not just so the kids could touch the only internal combustion engine they might ever see. It was also for the view. From the top of the dunes we could see the people of the young settlement below, putting their small fishing boats out to sea.

I stopped at the top of the path to fill my lungs deeply of the salty air, and to look north at the billowing patched yellow sails on the offing in the day's first light. But the children were patient for only so long. They started tugging and calling me, until we all went running down the face of the dune, spewing sand and laughing all the way. Half of the children would have given the dunes another run if I'd been inclined to let them.

At the docks, the path intersected with the beach trail. To the left were several temporary shacks, haphazardly occupied. To the right was our destination, the first building they had built here, over a decade ago, the little open chapel. I made my way toward it, and the familiar worn wooden benches.

Seashells and sand underfoot, we took our seats. The path wound crookedly on past the benches, through the beach grass, and was lost to sight far away where a huge slab of rock, the 'jump-off', jutted several hundred meters out into the bay.

I wondered if they had any idea why we had come here–what we had come to talk about. I wondered if I had the will to go through with it, remembering the times I had tried in the past, and failed.

"I was as high as the western cliffs"

"Tell us the story about the land bein' all ice Miss Willow," said little Greann as she squirmed on the bench, between two older siblings.

I'd grown used to this younger generation calling me either 'Miss Willow', or Teacher, as I'd gotten used to the furtive glances at the two claw marks, from my neck to my jaw line.

"And about the long boards you wore on your feet, to slide on the snow!" Chimed Vouy.

"Skis," I said laughing. "We've got all morning kid-dos, but I don't think it'll be enough time. Might take a few days in fact, because I'm going to tell you the story right from the beginning. Going to put it all together for you."

"You mean about the gold cave?"

"Oh, before that." I took a deep breath. *Finally, it's time to tell them of the world they never knew.*

"Way back when I's just a little older than you are now, people moved on the water with boats that didn't use oars or sails or wind." I pointed to the receding vessels. "They had what's called a motor. In our civilization, a motor took the place of sails, but it didn't look anything like them."

I reminded them about the stop at the top of the dunes—how I'd had them all make their best guesses at what kind of a thing was a Jackson 'Muck-Raker'. There were a few comments about the disagreeable oil smell, and a lot of wild speculation about what the outboard was for. Indeed, the motor still stank up close, after a decade and a half, but no one knew why.

I was glad to be sitting down. When it came right down to it, I was feeling an odd vertigo, like stumbling backward through time. "It was like, in the world I lived in, which actually this is still the same world—planet, of course—before everything changed, it was like, you'd wanna take time out for a breather—time out to smell the roses, but you knew that when you started sniffin', the clock wouldn't quit tickin'."

I had a sudden sinking feeling that I didn't even know how to begin, and was sure it showed. I found myself relying upon the reassurances I'd worked to internalize to get ready for this day. The biggest one was my confidence that the children would not be harmed, and would do no harm, by the harsh information my story would impart. I also sought youthful support for my idea of building and outfitting a trio of small craft, to sail to the mainland.

"That clock is another thing you don't have here, the idea of chopping up the day into pieces. Your people just do what they need to do, when they need to do it." I remembered the crowded impatient sidewalks of Altalanta, and almost wished to be back there, this was not starting out so good.

Once I got my momentum though, the history went on for hours. I proceeded to tell the children about submarines, and nuclear power, and factories, and money, and cars. The kids sat around munching on nuts and dried fruits, and encouraging me with their ceaseless questions.

I couldn't actually begin to tell them how I ended up on their island, without properly setting the world stage.

I told them of cavemen, of tribesmen, of gypsies, of monks, punks, pilots, and of war–this knowledge of war being personal. Some of this was old news to some of them, but I was giving them a living context, in myself.

The older children kept up with my more detailed explanations. They listened, not in awe, but with much interest, about fossil fuel, computer chips, and jets. "Imagine looking up at the sky, at any given moment, to see it crisscrossed by trails of vapor exhaust, contrails that hang in the air for long after the airliners have passed over."

Their faces as I told them of the last decades of the twenty-first century, only showed doubt when I touched on the subjects of space exploration, gang violence, oil spills, and robotics. *But Miss Willow wouldn't lie. Would I?*

". . . and a small exploratory mission off the island," I said, "would provide proof,"

That last remark was one I'd found myself repeating more and more over the years. There was no reason not to go. I didn't think that these people, whose ancestors had taken their whole population into an unknown plane of existence, could be afraid to sail over the horizon, but I wondered sometimes.

My throat was getting tired. I'd only just begun what would be a necessarily long and complicated account. These children were used to holding onto things in their heads. Still, it seemed uncanny to me how good they were at remembering word for word, the things I had told them since getting to know them.

With the sun up high in the sky, I was thinking how good a little nap in the shade would feel, when looking up, I saw Xoqueicue walking down the path carrying a basket on his back. I knew he was in the area today, and he must have heard that I'd be here also.

He was moving so gracefully that it took me a few seconds to realize that he was walking backwards. He sat the basket of breads and cheese and new wvintu down in the midst of the children, who made short work of the goods.

"You've probably all been wanting to hike down to the jump-off spot I told you about," I said to the kids after they finished eating. "I did promise this wasn't going to be all lessons. I'd love to talk your little ears off all day . . . but the rest can wait until tomorrow." To my pleasant surprise, a chorus of mutiny arose around me.

"No no. You all need a break, and if you don't, I do," I laughed. "Meera, you're in charge. Don't go beyond the jump-off. And come back *before* you're ready for supper so we can get back early enough." I knew I could rely on her to appoint a lifeguard or two, and to make everyone wait a few minutes, since we'd just eaten.

"Oh! Almost forgot," I said as I pulled a small capsule from my vest pocket. "You just go like this." I twisted the silver device and pulled either end–it telescoped to the length of my forearm. "Stick it in the water, like I showed you before."

I handed the gadget to Meera. The normally shy girl took it as if I were handing her Excalibur. That would ward off sharks and such. Half the kids had comrings too, so I wasn't worried. Some of them still seemed to want to hang around. I was about to press them off–I wanted to talk to Xoqueicue about something, in private.

"That thing will help," said Xoqueicue, "but do stay on this side."

Soon the children took the hint. Not however, without a few singsong jests about the two of us being more than 'in like' with each other, thrown back over the shoulders of the tweenage girls, Greeann and Ardonna.

"Jealous?" I hollered after them.

"Eew yuck!" Their high laughter trailed after them as they hurried off.

Xoqueicue made a call to Harmyn, and asked if he would train one of his vid-cells on the jump-off. The Aderans didn't have many children, but they took great pride in the ones they did. Every child was every adult's responsibility. Harmyn said the surveillance system was experiencing some inexplicable glitches, but he'd see what he could do.

On the bench gazing out over the gentle waves, I saw the birds and the cloudless horizon, but my mind's eye was seeing differently. Being near Xoqueicue had a strange effect on me sometimes. An inner sense of quietude overtook my soul.

"So sister," whispered Xoqueicue, "what did you learn from the children this beautiful morning?"

"Ha ha! I think by some slight chance I may have taught *them* something today."

"Oh, and what could a grey-haired old-worlder, have to teach that the little people should want to learn?" he asked in a jesting voice. "And, why is she so intent in passing on her knowledge of the time before?"

I'd found two grey hairs in my comb that morning, but was too stubborn to give Xoqueicue the satisfaction that he'd correctly read my lingering concern. "The kids have got to know what has passed, or they'll have no idea what to do with their future. I'm telling them about the world, how it was before all the shit hit the fan."

For a time we sat in silence, letting the waves speak for us. My consciousness began to drift out over the slowly swirling currents of the bay. ". . . how the world was before the comet."

I was enjoying a most exhilarating feeling of expansion and weightlessness. I knew from past experience, what was happening–what he was doing to my energy field. He tapped his toe three times, and I took the cue. Following his gaze, I saw the diminishing sailboats on the horizon and picked out the one he was watching.

With reluctant effort, I surrendered my train of thought.

We followed the receding sail with our eyes as it disappeared under the skyline. The Far Seers considered it an act to gain personal power, for two or more people to gaze upon something together as it left their field of view.

At last I couldn't help myself. "And anyway, my hair's not grey–two strands, and suddenly I'm catching up to you?!?"

He looked amused. "You should see how you look to your other self."

I was about to ask what he meant by that, but he patted his chest, and touched two fingers under his chin, which meant that we should try to engage in Iorgov–a form of meditation. I decided to indulge him for the time being.

"I've brought you a gift," he said after awhile. "It's in here." He handed me a polished yellow crystal of Quartz. I held the small crystal in the palm of my hand, felt it pulsing with energy–felt its vibrations seeping into my consciousness.

Compared to some on the leading council, or some of the old recluses out in the island's wilds, Xoqueicue may not have considered himself much of a Far Seer, but I did. In the past, his energetic manipulations of my consciousness had left me feeling weak in the knees–scattered, and crazed . . . and enlightened.

I closed my eyes. It felt as if time and space were trading places, so that time was on the outside, and space was on the inside. My consciousness slipped through a crack between them, and started to float free.

Xoqueicue whispered something in the spinning timelessness, keeping me from getting lost, telling me to gather my memories of the morning's story. This was a technique called Orgo Vordem, or 'sowing the past'. I'd done it once before with the guidance of the village singers, and twice by myself while dreaming. I could feel my energy fibers reaching out like tendrils, pulling in the history I'd spoken of to the children.

I had a feeling that the crystal was only part of the gift. Orgo Vordem was a way to duplicate the residual power of one's experiences–so that you could surrender the replicas, but keep the originals. As it was explained to me, the Great Spirit would take a trade. The result was that by storing enough of the by-product of the powerful practice, one could achieve things that seemed like magic.

I sensed that Xoqueicue was helping to boost my vibrations for something transcendental. My mind was rising up and out, growing, spinning, gathering energy. There was a moment's eternity of tension, like a bubble about to burst. Xoqueicue whispered, "Let it go now . . . give it back, for your freedom."

I felt his hand at the middle of my back, and realized I'd been holding my breath. I opened up with an enormous exhale, scattering the glowing seeds of my memories.

I don't remember opening my eyes, but I could suddenly see everything around me. I looked up and saw the sun and sky, the high noon moon, a cloud in bloom. I could see to either side, as if my eyes had moved on my face. Below were the yellow sails on the water.

I was surrounded by sky, and my arms stretched to become wings, spreading out to catch the wind. I pointed my beak to the sun, and gave an exultant cry before folding my wings, and taking a sharp dive. I made a swoop into the wind and regained some altitude. In a long slow circle I turned back around, so the island was below me. Again I made a dive, headlong into the warm breeze. The wind slid smoothly over my feathers. Ascending again, I saw my old rowboat atop the dunes, and was reminded of my near death, and of the silver cord.

In the slopes just above the beach, I made out the sod covered round buildings of the island people, saw some of the tiny figures in their gardens. I was as high as the western cliffs to my right. To the left were the children, like ants, leaping out as high as and as far as they could, to plunge into the warm waters below the jump-off. Directly below me was the beach chapel and the benches, where Xoqueicue sat . . . alone.

But, where am I?!

I looked quickly to each side, up the beach paths, behind the small chapel, in the water by the dock, worried that my body may have wandered off without my mind, and fallen in.

I looked all around as I slowed my descent. Soaring . . . circling . . . diving . . . nightmare dreaming . . . silently screaming. Yet, I was nowhere in sight.

It's not a dream! Descending, descending, I caught Xoqueicue's eye. He locked his gaze on mine for a moment, filling me with his confidence.

Looking back at the bench, I saw myself materialize, and grow solid.

I looked up into my other eyes, bird's eyes, only meters away, just as they faded out of existence. In an instant of pain and blackness it was over, and I was back in my head again, looking up at the sky.

"Nice," Xoqueicue said. He was close beside me, steadying me with his arms around my shoulders. He seemed deep in thought. "You may just live after all." He smiled, then touched his forehead gingerly to mine as he got up to go. He seemed unsteady.

But I barely heard him. I felt like I would fly apart into a million pieces. I leaped up on the bench, ecstatic, and spun around with my arms out like a bird. "I was flying!"

This brought a hearty laugh from the man who had just given me something beyond price. I felt my heart would burst, and I leaped from the bench. Laughing, he caught me like I was a child, and spun me around twice before we fell to the ground.

"I was flying! Why can't I do that by myself–and wh-where was my body?" He gave me the look I knew all too well. It meant that I had my own answers within. "Always stupid thoughts in my head, seem to come from nowhere. I can understand it but—"

"I've told you, you will have all your answers someday," he said as he helped me up. We brushed the sand off each other with the familiarity of lovers, though we had never been.

I motioned to the bench. "Can you stay for a while Cho, and talk? There's something I've been wanting to say."

Xoqueicue was back on the bench in a heartbeat. We sat there awhile as I searched his eyes for the warmth I always found. I tried several times to get it out, but between the lingering excitement of being a bird, and my own doubts about what I wanted to say, I was tongue-tied.

"You grow restless here, on Adera," he said, with his usual uncanny insight.

"Don't get me wrong," I said. "Your people's culture does more than just appeal to me, and that flying trick is out

of this world. It's just that I never really felt at home anywhere for long. Hell, even since I've been here, I've moved
six times, if you count my very first camp." I hooked my
thumb over my shoulder up at the dunes behind us.

Xoqueicue smiled. "You've told me a lot about the
physical differences between our life here on the island, and
the world you left behind. What about the cultural differences?"

"Left behind?" I let it suffice. "Our society had more
than a few very wrong, but deeply entrenched ideas. Ideas
that while you are in the midst of living them," I shrugged,
"you just go along with. Now I see them for what they were."
My gaze was directed out over the murmuring surf, but inside, I was looking back over the years to what I could only
call 'the time before'.

"Names for instance. We all begin mostly in harmo-
ny with the human family, in our mother's belly. When we
come away from that state of union, they tag you with two or
three names, as if personal identity was the great goal. And
that's just the beginning of a life nurtured on contradiction.

"You learn to live walking the edge of a knife. Too
much individuality, and you fall off one side, too much de-
pendence on community, and you fall off the other. Your
people here seem to avoid that."

Xoqueicue seemed to be trying to realize this last
idea. "But we all have names here too, and from what I understand, men have used names to tell each other apart for as
far back as we could call ourselves men. It's a function that
has its usefulness."

"Yeah, I know, it's just that you don't attach as much
importance here to a person's 'distinguishability'–that's
probably not a real word–their absolute identity I mean. For
one thing, you don't give surnames.

"In 'the time before' we were all infused with this
notion that we could conquer our mortality if our names lived
on, after our body, you know. This idea poisoned our children, but it was perpetuated through them too, in generation
after generation. Our children had to shoulder not just the
weight of our expectations for them, but also of-of *our* very
survival.

"Maybe I shouldn't talk, because I never had children. But I was one once, so . . ."

"And you're a woman. Didn't you say women surrendered their names, when they were *mated?*"

"Married," I corrected with a chuckle. "For a woman in our society it was the common expectation that she would die–symbolically that is–to have her husband's last name. The children she would carry, would bear his family name. Maybe *mated* is the right word."

Xoqueicue looked as if he thought this idea was crazy. "Would the men not surrender their names instead?"

"It'd be healthier if we would all surrender our names, be as anonymous as the animals, to free ourselves of erroneous human values. I think I can claim to have gained that much insight from my time alone in the wild."

"Interesting concept," he said.

"Names have the power to warp everything we do if we just do it to become known, rather than to just do it. But no, we want to outlive our bodies."

Xoqueicue nodded. "Cooperative effort is also in man's nature," he said. "So is expression of our creative drive. But these things are their own rewards."

"That kind of thinking wouldn't have worked before. The national focus was on money, and what it could buy of course. And mostly what it bought–leisure times, retirements, distractions and amusements–was the exact opposite of the hard work used to make the money. And if you didn't have enough money, you found a way to get someone else to make it for you."

"Was work such drudgery?"

"I don't know if I ever told you, but my great grandma was born a slave."

Xoqueicue wore a grim expression, "No, you haven't. But from all you've ever told me about your civilization's capitalist leanings, it convinces me that it was like a collective hypnotism . . . or a willful forgetfulness that turned brother against brother, and rewarded the one for slighting the other."

"And I was right there with them, till I 'fell out', I see now though, that with the right tools and the right intent, life can be so much more."

"You still worry though," he said, "that it could all go wrong here, or that some invader could bring us low."

"It, we, ruined so many good things. And most of the time, there was at least one glaring warning sign. We've done a lot of damage in our long domination of this planet—starting with killing off the mammoth, and the giant sloth, and probably a hundred other species larger than us. That's sad enough, maybe as much because it didn't have to happen for us to survive as a race, as because we didn't have the wisdom and the respect to stop it.

"But when the warning signs are everywhere, be-cause we can safely predict the failure of, oh I don't know—the stability of the world's climate! Or a comet from out of the blue—It's just so stupid!"

Xoqueicue interjected, "was stupid." A young couple walked by, hand in hand. I hadn't seen them since they were kids, in Harth. I wouldn't have expected the two to hit it off.

"They work for Harmyn," he said. I watched them with a silent yearning, as they made their way up the steps of the little stone beachside chapel.

"I'm interested to know what effect it—capitalism—had on art. At its best, art is an affirmation of the joy of life," he said.

I just shook my head at him. "Well, I guess you can't know everything can you? What effect do you think it had?" I didn't pause long enough to let him answer "It was good and bad, mostly bad."

"And, religion?"

I laughed out loud at this. Religion was a favorite subject of his. I knew that our practice of the Far Sight was considered neither a religion nor an art—it was something in between. But I was sure that in the millennia since the Far Seer's departure, the world had seen the worst sides of reli-gion in almost every one it had tried. "Before I came here, I'd have sworn that our race was the worst of evolution's products, not only were we bent on screwing it all up for our-selves, we had to try to muck it up for as many other of the planet's children as possible in the process.

"We took one of evolution's mandates—survival of the fittest—and turned it into a slogan."

He was shaking his head, "That doesn't leave much room for symbiosis . . . or peace . . . or potential for meaning-ful progress. You've got to have nature's balance. Close as you can get, you know."

We spoke for a while longer about the world I'd left. By the time we were done he was almost in tears. I'd never before told him what I knew of the worst of mankind's ills, toward the end. It was my turn to offer solace, and I couldn't think of any.

"I shouldn't have said anything. You . . . I . . . Hey, cheer up Cho. There's always the future."

"The future? It is chewed and devoured by the present, digested by the past and, like used food," he made a loud fart, "it's history." We both laughed.

"I'm glad you're downwind. Shall we go find the kids?"

"I shouldn't. I want to get the results from the programs we've been working on here. And that means an evening with Harmyn and his machines, and his wild theories." He took my hand. "Look, Willow . . . I want to know too, maybe as badly as you do. All we can do for now is, try to be ready, and when the day comes, we will take it."

He waved and started off, but I called him back. "I've always been meaning to ask," I said, and gestured up at the dunes, "about the stone man—the giant statue thing. Are they ever going to put it back up?"

He looked at me blankly.

"It was up top there. Looked like this." I took a stance facing the bay with my feet apart and my left arm out to the side, but still he showed no hint of recognition. "Well it was there when I came. Then it fell."

He shook his head.

"I figured if anyone would know about it, you would. Well, good luck with Harmyn. Guess I better round up the kids." *Should've known they wouldn't come back on their own.*

As I walked down the beach path to the jump-off, I thought about how I'd especially enjoyed enlightening the little folks about the internet since it was, at its most basic, an attempt to do with technology what these kids were learning to do with their minds, and their wills.

Most of my story would seem completely alien to the children, so I was giving them a lot of background first. Tomorrow I would tell them about countries, and politicians, and soldiers. Tomorrow I would tell them of dollars and yen, of cocaine and colas—about UFOs and OBEs and IBMs and the CIA. Tomorrow they would learn about the once modern world's moral code, and all its various conflicting laws; being a set of ever more complicated and unnatural rules, which too often drove people to break the rules, with ever more extreme and unnatural acts, calling for the rule makers to tack-on and tinker with the edifice of compiled law, like a paper tower of Babel.

That night, I lost track of how many times I had to force myself to quit thinking, when I should've been sleeping.

WAR AND WARMTH

I fought in the second Americon Civil War at nineteen; the war between the Demolicrats and the Republican'ts.

The snow came diagonally into the clearing, driven on stiff winds. The hard flakes stung my cheeks. Tree tops swayed as the snow they had collected was again taken up by the wind. "Yeh've got to take off your shirt," said Tuva.

"Then I ain't doing it."

"Yer pants too." His voice, heavy though it was with his guttural Ivik-Tuvic accent, held a strange mixture of confidence and shyness.

"Then I'm *def*-initely not!"

"Well, how do you expect it to work?" Tuva looked at me expectantly. "I'm just trying to teach you," he said. "I thought you wanted to learn this."

"I did, but—"

"That's why we came out here, right?"

The worsening weather worried me. *If this is just a way to get to see my stuff, I'll . . .*

But a change of thought was coming over me. *I might be wasting a rare chance.*

"Besides, this isn't so bad. Where I come from we call—"

"Shove it," I said. The Ivik-Tuvic had a hundred words for different snows, nine of which were just for different kinds of sleet. I could never remember them because I couldn't pronounce some of the strange sounds 'the people' used to pass for speech.

"I'll do it."

He looked surprised, and pleased. I did trust him after all, probably more than any of the other guys on base. And I liked him, even for all his bizarre ways and stories. He had offered to show this technique, this rite, to any of us. So far, I was the only one to take him up on it. I was a little proud of that–this girl from Blakely getting one up on the big tough men.

"You keep your boots on of course–an yer delikits, *if you want.*"

I just rolled my eyes at him. I'd had an idea it might involve something like this, so I'd worn my lucky boxers and a sports-bra.

He shrugged and splayed his hands. "What?! I've got a girl back home."

"I sure hope she's keeping your igloo warm," I said, and started to undress.

An impetuous teenage prank involving a three-mile stretch of mailboxes along a country road, my boyfriend, some cheap beer, and a baseball bat, led to my being 'persuaded' into the army. Geoffrey got off with 10 months jail. Now somehow, here I was getting lessons in the fine art of being one with the cold; the rite of Cooh Kai.

This wasn't exactly why the army hired these northernmost of Alas Ka's natives. They were to teach us survival techniques yes, but this was something more, something he'd learned as a child, above the farthest reaches of the cold fingers of the Titan Mountains.

Tuva had been an orphaned foundling–raised in the wild north by one of the last of the Ivik-Tuvik Shamans, a harsh old man by the sound of it. He and his wife Muckamoot had found the toddler frozen to the spot where he had fallen, unnoticed, off the back of his parent's snow-machine. They rescued the boy and warmed him. Muckamoot chewed some dried seal meat for little Tuva while the old man followed the trail to where he found the crevasse, and at the bottom, the sled and the frozen parents, and the whiskey bottle.

And so, Tuva came to be raised in the old ways of his people, for which he was grateful, despite the often off-color jokes he told about his adopted parents.

I followed him at a vigorous pace over several kilometers of deep snow, adjusting my technique with the snowshoes slightly to keep the powder from spewing the backs of my bare legs. I was also aware of some internal adjustment, more than just my body's natural defense against the cold. There was a difference in me on a deeper level. I felt a connection beyond the physical, an awakening of something spiritual that left me speechless for hours afterward.

A week later. North of the Laurentian border.

The hardest part about Army life was reconciling my young idealistic beliefs, with the aims of war. The expediency of war–this one at least–was as much about stereotyping, as it was about quelling society's moral ills. I guessed they called it a civil war because it was fought by, for, and against civilians.

I was forced into the army to fight the rising tide of free-militia anti-government violence. *What the heck, take care of this little fuss, then get on with my life.*

It was to be a short war, but win or lose, it was a fight that the U.S.&A. couldn't afford.

After I was 'drafted', all the hell in the world broke loose. We were pushed through boot-camp. Bad news and tough fighting were the twin demons of my new universe. My heart wasn't in it. Nevertheless, I tried to tell myself that at least while we were at it, the government had the good sense to take out the worst of the degenerates, along with the militia boys.

We soldiers were supposed to think of ourselves as a special sort of society. What a sad joke. On the inside, it was all discipline and alcohol, rigidity and reconciliation, routine and the occasional rape.

But on the outside, on the whole, it was just as bad.

A dozen doomsday subcultures had meanwhile sprung up out of the relics of old prophecies built on the idea that society was in some new phase of very fast decline. Some were high minded, some just high. Some were anarchic, and wrought much anonymous havoc.

The necessary shortsightedness of war, blinded the people in power to the fact that what they were fighting for was a way of life that was utterly unsustainable, regardless of the fact that the doomsayers might be right. I didn't know what I wanted out of life, but certainly didn't want to consider as mine, the goals of this war, any war.

Even then, I was convinced that the best thing for Aerda would be for humankind to just do nothing. At least then, we wouldn't be ruining everything we claimed to love so much.

Toward the end of my time in the war, our platoon was dealing with a small band of renegade militia–one of our specialties. We were nicknamed the Foxhunters, and proud of it.

Actually, the good-ol-militia-boys were generally slack and unorganized, except for a few lunatic loners. The loners often went north into Laurentia. Unofficially, we were encouraged to go across to fetch them back, both by the Laurentians, and by our commanders. We weren't supposed to take our own sweet time about it, and they would limit our actions to simple small incursions. That, and the weather, made for some tension in our platoon.

The Laurentian people weren't exactly friendly to us, nor were they consistent. We could hang the militia boys if we liked, but they'd hide the draft dodgers. The Francolaurentians, after all, had a long history of opposition to any form of draft.

The border between our northern neighbor and us was a cakewalk, and their policy of harboring dodgers worked for them in two ways. First, it looked good to the Associated Nations. Second, it amounted to a 'brain gain' since many of the dodgers were college educated.

While the militia boys were holed up in an old lumber camp to the north, Tuva was teaching me how to accept the cold–*to be one with it.*

We had volunteered together for the re-con, thinking that if the opportunity arose, he could continue my lessons. "With any luck, we'll get stuck out in Vook Shavig, the big blizzard," he said enthusiastically.

The going was good, the weather report had been good, we were half a klick from our turnaround. "Don't think it's going to happen," I said with mock disappointment.

Whether we're fighting in it or not, war affects every one of us—every dollar spent, every oilfield bombed, every child maimed, every secret buried, every 'expedient action', and every hometown hero fallen—we own it all.

With one hand clutching the M-16, the other holding up my pants, I ran up the hill as fast as the deep snow would allow.

As the bullets flew around us, I dodged behind the large downed tree and laid down cover fire, as Tuva ran to my position. The militia guy below us lurched crookedly backward. I took a quick glance to the left, about to tell Tuva that I had a hunch I'd gotten the guy, but Tuva was lying crookedly behind the big log, already bleeding to death from his face.

I covered his body with mine, as if I could protect him, and had a momentary loss of identity, sobbing hysterically for several minutes, until a grim calm finally forced itself over me. There was nothing to do for him.

I buttoned up my pants, and made hasty preparations to vacate the area before the others—there would be others—showed up to hunt the huntress.

I was on my way back to my platoon when I found the stuffing coming out of two bullet holes in the fold of my coat under my left armpit. When I realized how close I had come to dying for my country, I closed my ears to the call of duty, and let my feet turn my skis around in their tracks.

The coming snow would help—the trick would be to leave no side trail, when and where I picked to exit-stage-left. I was sure that Tuva had pushed the distress call when the shooting started. With any luck I could slip away, and our guys would meet the bad guys, and in the resulting chaos, I could make a double getaway. *F**k 'em all.*

I had all I needed to survive, and the coming spring was close. A weeklong thaw soon melted most of the snow. Weather in the midst of worldwide climate change does funny stuff. The next week, blizzards blanketed the rugged landscape in white, deep as I was tall, pristine, beautiful.

For six weeks I lived on what I could gather, shoot, or steal as I journeyed north and west. A diet of draccoon, the particularly vicious, six legged, winged 'rat' common to the wild lands bordering the Tuke-on, was not as tasty it was necessary. It was more a case of eat or be eaten, than a diet.

I rarely stayed two nights in the same place—I knew the Foxhunters—knew what they did to my kind.

"A diet of draccoon"

There was an expectancy on the winds.

With four hundred kilometers or so of the vast beautiful Laurentian wilderness behind me, I finally traveled with a lighter heart. I'd passed west through half of the middle part when I heard the first blackbird.

I was still using the skis, but in the last week, I'd come to more than a few spots where I had to take them off for crossing large bare brown patches.

While crossing one of the final ridges before the mountains, I caught the faint scent of a wood fire. I'd already made up my mind to try to find somewhere soon to settle for awhile. I certainly wasn't going mountain climbing due west, and didn't want to go any further north, into the great tundra. I couldn't see the smoke, but had a feeling about this wind-borne hint of nearby civilization, so I followed my nose.

I finally decided to investigate it in the morning, as it was getting late. I needed enough time before dark to set up camp, which meant finding a spot in the next fifteen minutes.

There was still up to a meter of snow in most areas where drifts had accumulated. It was spring, but I didn't want to be up on the bare ridge with the way the wind was picking up. I left the high ground where a narrow canyon split the landscape, and pinpointed my position on the map. It was home to the headwaters of Yono Creek.

I snowplowed with the skis to a stop a respectable distance back from the ledge. These drifts had been known to sheer off underfoot, and take the foolish for the ride of their lives.

Just below me was the source of the smoke, a cabin in the shelter of the pines. A thin grey snake's tongue tested the air above the stone chimney, and was quickly lost in the deep blue above the gently swaying spruces.

I couldn't think of a good reason to wait until morning. Call it a woman's intuition, but I sensed I'd be staying the night in the cabin below. Of course, the feeling was tempered by the few accounts I'd heard of north-woods hospitality, and possibly by a dose of my own return to myself. I was ever less the Army's prey with each passing week, as I let the drills and regimentation fall away. And, as I was able, I had even replaced the outfit of war I had worn when I deserted. Now, I was just another north-country lady, from a distance anyway.

I didn't think there were many of my color around these parts though, and there would be no one up here who would speak quite like me, *eh*. I doubted that I could pass myself off as a tourist. A guy would have an easier time saying he was a dodger. They didn't technically draft women. However, I was special–if special meant unruly. *Maybe they won't ask.*

I wasn't against using my so-called 'feminine wiles'. Just hadn't had to yet.

The logs of the cabin were massive. Each wall was made of only three logs, but even the top one was as big around as a pregnant pony.

I took my time approaching the porch. I noted the most recent tracks were of big boots, small shuffling steps– coming from a building down the path and going straight up the porch steps. Cleaning the snow off my skis, I clacked them loudly together. *Hello! I'm here.* Expectant echoes in my head of a little yapping dog, or a hearty 'Hullo who's thar,' died away under the rising breezes.

The porch encompassed the front half of the cabin. I stomped my snowy boots and rattled the skis noisily into the rack beside the front door, alongside another pair. The door was rugged, like everything else.

I knocked. Waited. Moaning winds gave the only answer.

Maybe there's a back door. I'd seen a little outhouse back there. I knocked louder. And again, longer. *Maybe they're deaf.* I depressed the door latch, and pushed enough to get my face inside. Warmth, and a manly lived-in odor, squeezed out as I hollered in, "HELLO . . . I'm coming in."

All in all, I had gone thirty five days without talking to another human being.

The man lay sprawled before the hearth. He was dressed in long johns and boots. Most of his body was on the bearskin rug, but the side of his face was pressed into the hardwood floor in a pool of spittle. I could see his chest rising and falling slowly.

His left eye turned imploringly toward me.

"'I call unto even the Lord of all Hell, and all his wretched demons, to witness my oath this day, and even to follow on my heels, though they will not darken the path before me! Neither man nor mountain nor Devil will stand in my way!' Vowed Haigar the—."

I stopped when a movement from across the hearth caught my eye. I looked up from the page to see he had slumped forward in the stuffed chair, and was drooling into the cocoon of blankets. I was reading to him from Bernard Graham's Mythica series, the second volume. I guessed he had heard enough. *Poor old guy.* I closed the book, marking the page with a strip of birch bark, and stood to place it back on the shelves behind me.

My pity was soon replaced by a numbing sense of duty when I caught a whiff of what he'd done in his make-shift diaper.

In the week that I had been there, I'd come to learn a lot about the old caretaker–his name was Jacques. I'd gone through the place from top to bottom a couple times, first to look for medicines he might need, not realizing that he'd had a stroke.

I was no nurse. All I could do for him was to make him comfortable, try to feed him and get some water down his throat, change his ass from time to time, and read from the cabin's eclectic collection of books–a third of which were in English.

It had been a busy week. My own standards for cleanliness in a place to live were slightly higher than Jac-ques'–I spent a couple hours a day, one room at a time bring-ing the cabin up to them. Caring for the old caretaker took another couple hours a day, and filling his shoes as the newly self-appointed caretaker took a couple more.

I also spent a fair amount of time going through each of the buildings–six in all, including the little outhouse be-hind the cabin, and the two-holer down the slope at the place's main base of operations.

Three large buildings below the cabin were obvious-ly waiting for the arrival of a work-crew. At first, I thought the place was maybe a hunting and fishing camp when I opened the door to the dorm-style workman's quarters. There would be good hunting no doubt, and had been, as was ap-parent by the mounted trophies.

The other two buildings were all business, filled with equipment and supplies, and small explosives. It was a min-ing camp. They were digging deep in Mother for gold. I myself never much understood the madness over the soft yellow metal.

A perusal of the paperwork in the desk in the little corner office of the big warehouse confirmed that mining operations here would soon resume. Most of the writing was in French, and my single semester in high school had hardly prepared me for this, but by the end of the week, with practice, it was coming back to me.

Jacques was getting progressively worse, but the two radios on his desk in the cabin got me to thinking. I had them both turned on, after putting Jacques on the cot I'd made up for him next to the wood stove. One radio was a shortwave–easy enough to figure out, and so I had a small link to the outside world, after leaving it almost two months before.

The other radio was a bit more complicated, but I finally found the instruction booklet underneath it. I was glad to see that it was printed in three languages, including English. Call letters for Jacques' employers were penciled in on the last page, top right corner.

When the man who owned the mine arrived, he came with a paramedic on board. He showed his appreciation for the preparations I'd made after finding Jacques. My call had come too late to save him though. He died in the plane, before they made it back to civilization.

Martin didn't ask about my history, and I stayed on to work for him, continuing to fill old Jacques' shoes. I even worked the mine occasionally, along with the other crew. The work was hard, but rewarding in its own way.

Come fall, it seemed only natural to stay on for winter. As caretaker, I wasn't expected to do any mining on my own, just ward off lions and tigers and bears and looters–*takes one to know one*–and not get killed in the process.

The pay was good enough. I took half of it in gold as an advance. All the refinery equipment had been put to bed for the winter. The little cabin had been stocked and fortified for the five months ahead. The rest of the crew had already left.

"You've got *feu d'artifice* girl," said Martin as we waited by the lake for the last plane.

"Fireworks?" I wondered momentarily if he was referring to the explosives.

He placed two fingers on my sternum and nodded. "Here."

Whatever it meant, I could see he had said it as a compliment.

The plane was clearing the ridge. "Keep those batteries up, and don't you hesitate to use the radio if anything–happens." He nodded at the plane. "Be back up here in under four hours."

"What if I just want to chat a bit?"

"Anytime Willow. Anytime. You're *famille* now."

I saw his sincerity and I hugged him for a moment, letting the closeness refresh and stir my soul. "Figure I'll check-in twice a week anyway. Tuesdays and Fridays?"

"Sure, what time eh?"

"Noon?" We were walking out onto the dock single file, carrying his bags.

"Noon it is then," he shouted over the drone of the plane's dying engines. "Did I mention we're going to rig up a satellite receiver next season? The power system will handle it. Just a matter of inviting eh-um, how you say *tech geek*, up here who can hook it all up right."

"Yep." The plane was slowing to a stop at the end of the dock.

"You don't sound too excited. Most kids would have to be hooked up to Space-face or something to stay the winter here."

"I'll live."

"Remember girl," he said as he stepped onto the plane, "get some sun when you can."

Almost involuntarily, I saluted him.

ICE AND FIRE

Astronomers estimate up to one hundred comets and more than two thousand asteroids, capable of causing a large scale extinction event. Just one of the things I learned from the cabin's extensive library. It was long ago, but if I remember correctly it was from a book called On the End, by Quilliam Richards.

I learned of the comet, named 'El Vaca' for the mountain top observatory where it was first discovered, while listening to the shortwave. I was switching back and forth through the stations, between chapters of one of his westerns on the old caretaker's birthday. The book must've been one of his favorites, judging by the tattered look of it. He would have been sixty-four, too young to die. At least he wasn't cold and alone at the end.

By the light of a kerosene lantern, I read aloud the exploits of good Cabin Jack and the treacherous Ketchum boys. Music from midway through the last century played quietly on the shortwave.

Periodic updates on El Vaca interrupted every station, and I kept turning the dial. *Either tell us if it's going to blast us to bits or pass us by. Til then, shaddup pardner, I am trying to read here. Or just shoot the damned thing out of the sky already.*

I heard that this was no ordinary comet, and that it was due to pass between Aerda and the moon, but with a reasonably comfortable margin of safety. El Vaca was not one of those flashy splashy comets. It hadn't even started to show its tail until a week before, when it was discovered, and since it was heading straight for us, we were actually lucky to see it when we did. Further, it was one of the deep space wanderer types that we shouldn't expect to see again for 400 years or more.

Then came the announcement that it had somehow been pulled off course, and it was falling inexorably into the planet's gravity well, contrary to all the scientific opinions money and influence could churn out. I finally put Cabin Jack down to listen in earnest. There were increasingly confused and alarming announcements, presumably on every station.

Pacing the floor, I was about to reach for the mike key of the big Com 40, when the dial jumped and the speaker croaked out my name. It was Martin.

"It's me," I said, ignoring the operator protocols. "What's going on Martin!?"

"Comet El Vaca seems to be circling Aerda," he said. "Or will anyway, before morni—" Static jumped out of the speaker between unintelligible snatches of words–some Martin's, some not.

The shortwave was spitting the same sorts of minced messages, so I quickly turned it down a bit. Again I clamped my hand around the mike, "Boss, Martin, I'm not reading you. Come again?" I paused. Nothing. I tried several more times without success.

My mind was racing to reassemble the bits of his words that *had* come through the static. I had definitely heard 'shelter'. They were taking shelter, or maybe I should take shelter.

The static on the shortwave cleared up long enough to catch, "—and while it's doubtful that a comet or meteorite could bump Aerda out of its orbit, it would be much more destructive than the first H-bomb that killed 100,000 people and dest— —blast wave would send a huge mushroom-cloud miles into the air, instantly burst the lungs of anyone within fifty miles, and start a series of powerful aerthquakes throughout the world.

"Scientists speculate that a hit such as the one we now face could even reverse our already destabilized planetary magnetic polarity." The announcer's voice quavered, which disturbed me more than the actual information, as he went on to describe what all might happen if the comet hit us. He ended his report with a statement of his love to his wife and children, 'if they were listening'.

Static crept in and drowned out the next report. I fiddled with the dial. *Come on you old piece of crap.* "—ong evidence supports the theory that a killer comet struck Aerda sixty-four million years ago. The ensuing death of almost all the vegetation on the planet caused the extinction of the dinosaurs! Any who survived the initial blast skulked around in unending darkness and slowly starved to death if they didn't free—" Static and noise played a maddening melody in the speakers.

I turned the dial again, hoping against hope that this was some sick joke. "—most devastating effects, were the calamities that ensued for months or years afterward. The cloud of dust and debris would have brought immediate darkness to the surrounding area. A week later, a growing band of high-borne dust, spread on stratospheric winds, would darken the same latitude as the explosion.

"Shortly, the entire planet might suffer perpetual winter. Sorry folks but it looks like this could be it for our sorry lot, and for those of you who just went out to get next year's summer clothes at a bargain, too bad."

Over the next hour, between the two radios, I was able to get a good idea of what was happening. But one by one, the stations I'd come to know around the world disappeared from the shortwave's dial. I tracked El Vaca's course by the radio stations I could no longer receive, and determined that it was headed my way.

Even if it was only going to circle the planet, as some were saying, it was still wreaking its havoc, spewing chunks of itself like some sputtering old god. *Maybe you will end the war.*

I began to consider another possibility. I imagined it up there like another moon. Evidently there were already a few 'captured' asteroids, invisible to the naked eye, orbiting Aerda–one of which was five kilometers wide. So why not a fire-spitting harbinger of doom.

By the time the comet would have passed over my location I had gone down into the mine as far as I could, not even knowing why, and then questioning my decision. *If it hits, I'm dead either way–buried down here, or vaped up there.*

I stayed in the mine for a day, just in case, only poking out a few times to see if anything looked different. Sensing no sign of danger, I went back to the cabin.

Both radios flickered on as I flipped their switches, but that was all. No amount of calling, or adjusting dials, or beating the things with the palms of my hands produced anything but dead static. I had a good idea of what it meant by then, and felt my blood begin to boil as I clenched my fists in desperate frustration.

The sound of the door slamming open was muted by the rising winds. I ran to the doorstep. *We can make wars like there's no f**king tomorrow, but we can't kill one God-damned comet!* I stormed outside and vented my useless rage, ranting at the stirring black clouds from the top of my lungs, until I was hoarse.

With each passing hour, I became surer that the comet had not come down, not all of it anyway. Something had happened though.

In 2008 in a remote sector of the Cyberian plains, a comet fragment collided with Aerda–only a fragment. The engineer of the Trans-Cyberian Express, six-hundred kilometers away, felt such a shock that he thought his train had exploded. At its epicenter, the blast leveled huge firs over four hundred square miles of forest, and wiped out most of the reindeer population of the area.

In 2059 a meteor plunged into the Castelorizen Sea, causing more than two dozen major shipwrecks as the resulting tsunami swept out in an eight hundred mile radius. The small island of Yuyindi, population two-hundred-sixty, was obliterated.

I hadn't felt anything more than a slight trembling, and I might've missed that, if I hadn't been waiting for the worst. I knew it must have been worse for certain other quarters of the globe, but the changes were harder to count in my world.

I had come to a few of my own conclusions about what had happened–a short list of opinions that is. The only thing I *knew,* was that there was the comet, and it had gotten pulled into a partial orbit. Getting into the realm of probabilities, I started with El Vaca's seemingly odd return to the void–it almost certainly should have crashed down upon us, and ended our existence once and for all.

For all their tenacious longevity, comets are basically fireflies, on a different scale. As long as they are winging around the solar system, they age very slowly, but they are fragile in their way. Gigantic balls of dirty ice–they lose a bit more of their essence with each inner space excursion. The sun takes its toll–hence the sometimes brilliant show that is the comet's signature, its 'flaming' tail.

It travels in its own halo of debris and dust, a glowing stream of shed fragments. The winging comet is continually leaving itself behind. Sometimes they hit another object, and the winner is determined mostly by size. More often, they fly by on the same basic elliptical plane, the narrow band in which almost all the sun's subjects circle. Some few comets have extremely distended orbits. Their flight can lead them far far away from the sun, across the paths of all the other members of the solar system.

When El Vaca came too close to us for comfort, it was not quite close enough to crash, but it was enough for our gravity to distort its integrity. As it circled, it shed bits of itself, making it lighter.

It would have been an awesome sight from outer space. Maybe it came in on Aerda's leading edge at such an angle that the effect was much the same as when the gravitational pull of the sun, coupled with a comet's speed, slingshots the comet back out to the cold fringes of space in an age old dance. Maybe the moon was in a position to help with a tug of its own gravitational force.

Some of its fragments did strike, and did raise clouds of millions of tons of dust. I could see the dust–taste it on the air, feel it as an extra teardrop in my eye. It was in the snow, and on my skin, as thick and possibly as toxic as any city smog.

My supplies of food, fuel, and winter clothes allowed me to survive, while the cabin was being buried under tons of snow. Books and crossword puzzles, and lots of sleep, kept cabin fever at bay.

When the snow topped the cabin's peak, I began to worry about smoke inhalation. *What if it goes over the chimney?* I added lengths of stove pipe, and improvised some rough duct work for ventilation through one window, up toward the darkened sky.

When I couldn't stand the seclusion and its attendant delusions anymore, I climbed and burrowed up out of the grand-daddy of all snowdrifts. It was now April, and still dusky all day, but the snow had developed several hard-packed layers that I thought I could stay on top of with the back-country skis.

I would make a trial run up onto the ridge–see what I could at high noon. As I did so, I couldn't help but think of Tuva's people, further north even than me. *Can y'all be surviving this?*

Waiting for a break in the weather, I finally decided to make tracks South when my supplies would last only another month. I packed what I could onto a sawed-off dog-sled, which I would pull.

I had to go on only the vaguest of information, regarding direction. There were no stars, and only a smudgy hint of the sun. My compass usually proved useless–a daily source of spinning and quivering disappointment. At least I could see well enough for a general southern progression for six or seven hours a day.

Two desperate weeks later. 100 Kilometers South.

I'd already gotten turned around a couple times–I'd lost a whole day backtracking. I had been skiing since the first hazy light of morning, and it was now getting late in the day. I could tell where the sun was by the faintest circle of light low in the western sky.

I had finally found a hint of civilization. I traveled along with the north-south power lines, hoping they were following a road–but all I could see of the poles above the snow was the top three or four meters, and the wires. I still had some food, but my water had run out the night before, which was most unfortunate since half of my foodstuff was dried goods.

I didn't want to make water by melting the snow. It may have been harmless for all I knew, but it didn't look or taste good. *Civilization's crowning anti-achievement; water you can't drink, as far as the eye can see.*

I looked for the exposed peak and chimney that marked the spot that was once a person's house. Then all I would have to do was dig down through the snow to a window and break in.

As I trudged along in the dark, pulling the sled, I thought back to how life had been before all of this extermination. Even as hard as it was, I sometimes wondered which was worse–this cold quiet lonely fight for survival, or the out of control bustling and bumbling of civilization.

The rhythmic sound of my skis made me remember long boot-camp marches with the rest of the company. I thought of the sergeants calling us worthless as dirt when one of us would fall, and there was some consolation knowing that I never had to be insulted by them again. But it was small comfort when tempered by the ironic thought that I was alive because of that very training.

Most of the time I just cleared my mind, and kept moving on automatic.

I had a good tent, but I'd been finding better lodgings and looting the further south I came. I'd even made an indulgent, though difficult, single-handed raid on a little town–what was left of it that is–Aubrey's Point, West Dakota. I regretted half the stuff I'd loaded onto the sled when I tried pulling it the next morning. Frustrated and cursing, I started tossing half of the stuff right back off, until I grabbed the gas can.

The old man had paddled me good one day, when I dumped the gas out of one of his cans, lucky me I hadn't put the match to it yet. He made me understand that it was not so much for the wasting of the money he'd spent, but for the ill effects on the environment, "our Aerda." Papa was always good about applying reason to our brains if he had to apply pain to our behinds. Our hearts lay in between, which is where he was aiming. So I couldn't bring myself to just toss the can.

Then I began to smile at the thought that, of course there would be a snowmobile somewhere in town, in some garage. *Might mean a day's digging.* As it turned out, I spent nearly two more cold hard days before finally finding a sled that would run. The decrepit old thing had one big ski in the middle and a doublewide track. I tied the rope of my sled to the hitch and we were off.

Back to the skis.

Most machines failed to start for me–the ones that did, weren't worth the trouble when they would break down shortly thereafter. I finally quit trying.

The shadowy silhouette of the Titan range stretched out against the dull glow to my right. I estimated forty-five minutes of 'grey-light' left. I saw a glint of something up ahead, so I got a closer look with my binoculars. What I saw a half kilometer away made me jump with joy–the roof and silo of an old barn. I scanned to either side, and dimly made out the peak of a house.

It wasn't too late to reach the place. I could almost feel the warmth of a good meal, and my bedroll.

On the heels of my joy came an old apprehension, born of the days I'd spent on the run from the Fox-hunters. Part of me hated to face another night because I feared the dreams that would come.

The worst dream was always the same, with me standing defiant but scared on the edge of a skyscraper, wind blowing my hair wild, and the Sarge threatening to lash me with a whip. The lights of the city below had all gone out. I could hear three voices. Sarge was calling me names. My father, who had been dead since I was eleven, would plead with my mother to make him stop.

Mama would say, "It's good for the girl, don't worry. Sometimes children need a good tongue lashing. She'll toughen right up, you'll see."

The sun was gone, and pitch black night was settling in as I made my way down through the top story window. I was too exhausted to do much but make myself comfortable in an easy chair by a warm fire.

Sleep came soon, lasted long, and so did the dream.

A month later and I still had the clunky old back-country skis with me, but I had recently taken to a different mode of travel–I found an old rowboat, with a creaky outboard that worked only half the time. The mighty Hexarkana river was going my way after all, so motor or no, I was happy to leave the trusty old dogsled at the riverside, and go with the flow.

After making my way south by keeping the dim distant Titans on my right, I was starting to see traces of the solar disc almost daily. I considered it more luck than anything that I had made it this far.

When I did find a house, there was often an air of abrupt abandonment. While I found this disturbing and confusing, it was also the reason I always came away with food, and whatever other supplies I might need.

There were sometimes storms that raged for two or three days on end, and there was nothing to do but curl up with candles and a good book, or rummage through the remnants of someone's life, but I could never bring myself to feel at home or at ease in any of the places that I came to. It was a race with the seasons. I wanted to beat summer to the coast. I took risks—was a tough girl—and pressed myself now, for the reward ahead. I didn't know what I even meant by that, *some great reward,* it was just a gut feeling that drove me onward.

Even in that frozen desolate wasteland I knew I had to stay alive in case there *was* someone else—had to keep believing that I was not the only one, which is all that kept me sane.

Nearing the little town of Echo, it was already dark, and the river was bad enough during the eight hours or so of half-light. I had to find a spot for the night. My map showed two bridges—apparently most of Echo was on the north side of the river—any vehicle traffic would use the highway bridge further down. The first one was for trains.

The bridge was a welcome sight—I really had to pee. I was hungry, and had a craving for fries and a burger, of all things. I could follow the railway into town, even though it was covered by snow.

The tracks would take me right through the north part of town. Somewhere in town there would almost certainly be a ways and means to rustle up some satisfaction for my over taxed metabolism.

It was a chore pulling the boat up out of the river, and trying to keep an eye out for danger. For the last week I had seen wolf tracks, and kills, and a pack of four coyotes–nature's cleanup crews. *Must be good business for them, all this.*

When I found their tracks and their scent there under the lee of the bridge, I un-holstered one of the pistols and got down on all fours to examine the tracks–I'd long since become accustomed to the dimness, and didn't want to use the lamps, for fear of attracting attention more than for conservation. The distant cousins, Lupus lupus and Canis latrans, had come through since the last snow. *Today then.*

Most of the tracks went parallel with the river for as far as I could see in the dark, but a few of the coyotes had padded away to where the bridge met solid ground.

I would be going up that way myself in a couple minutes.

After marking my territory–peeing next to the boat, and then tossing around a bit of the 'varmint' powder I'd picked up at the last Home-Sweet-Depot–I did a few stretches so my back wouldn't cramp. I changed boots, strapped the pack on, got clamped into the skis, and sidestepped up the bank.

On my way into town, I passed close to an old red barn with a big white arrow painted on the side toward the road. In large white letters above the arrow, was a single word, and two names, 'Mom. Andy's–Hobson'. I didn't have the first idea of its intended meaning, but I remembered seeing the same sort of message the day before, in the last town, and it had puzzled me that someone would paint 'Mom–Echo', over a MacDonald's billboard. Both messages had a big 'Z' under a directional arrow.

There I was on my way into the town of Echo, with the inkling that 'Z' was leaving directions for Mom to find him or her at Andy's, wherever that was.

It seemed odd to see knee-high road signs, but at least the snow wasn't over the rooftops here. My curiosity was stirring as I skied through town, looking for a likely spot to plunder and/or spend the night, when I found Hobson Street.

Still following the coyote tracks, I skied slowly down the middle of Hobson, bindings squeaking. The wind was softly stirring up a few flakes. The town seemed considerably larger in the dark than the standard little open dot my map suggested. According to the map legend, that dot meant 'population less than two thousand'.

This could take awhile.

So I swung off my nearly empty pack–I'd readied it at the boat in case I was to find 'irresistibles'–and dug out some Hurky's Jurky and a canteen.

Is Andy's a bar? Maybe it's a friend's house. Z is probably Zak. Does Ma know where Andy's is? Most likely.

It somehow seemed important, being the first confirmable sign I'd yet seen that somebody besides me had actually lived beyond the day the comet came. As I washed down the last bite of jerky, I made up my mind to spend only an hour unraveling this little mystery, if only to give me something to do.

So far, all I'd found since leaving the mine had only served to confuse me–plenty of burned out houses and other buildings, and a fair number still standing in good condition. Some of the places I'd been, had signs of fire within, usually with the look of having been hastily extinguished. Half of the places looked superficially plundered, and then abandoned. I hadn't found a single corpse. Nor had I found a clue as to where everyone had gone. *South I guess, like me.* I'd just waited longer.

Five minutes down Hobson, and I came to a house with a big blue gingham dress up a flag pole, and over the front door, a 'Z' in slashes of white paint.

The house was otherwise unremarkable–brown with white trim, two stories with a wide roofed-over side porch.

I stepped easily up onto the one bare corner of the porch's roof, where the snow had been swept clean by the March lion winds we were still getting, on May the first. The coyotes had been up there too. Their spoor was on top of the drift before me, still fresh. Their tracks had gone all around the house–but only *their* tracks. I jammed my knee into the bank of hard snow to make a step, from which I vaulted up.

I found I could budge the left-hand second story window. I pushed my face up to the glass and flipped the lamp switch for only a second. A flight of stairs issued down from a small landing.

I cleared away some snow to get a better grip. I tried several times before getting the window up high enough to jam my foot into the gap. I sat there for a second and got my breath, before kicking in enough snow to get my body through. I suppressed a vision from my wild-child high school years of climbing through Geoffrey's window. The last time I'd done that was the night of the perfect score; *Willow 10'–mailboxes of the white, rich, and judgmental, '0'. That's riigght.*

I slipped through to the landing and crouched to listen for a moment. It was utterly dark and there would be no adjusting of the eyes to that, so I flipped on the lamp at power level one. *Good enough.*

By this time, my standard procedure at a house was to go through it once quickly, top to bottom, noting anything interesting.

If I needed anything, I could usually find it one way or another at the first house I'd stop at. If not, I'd break into a store. The main thing I needed though, would invariably be a good night's sleep.

If I needed water, the handiest, and often the only reservoir, was the block of ice I would find in the cracked toilet tanks. A couple finishing blows with a hammer and the porcelain would fall away leaving a rectangular block of ice. If the tank *wasn't* frozen, I would know by the look and smell that someone had actually made some winterizing preparations with antifreeze. That was rare though, except in the places that turned out to be summer homes.

If I needed food there was usually something–I only went for unopened goods, and only stuff that handled being frozen. I burned a lot of calories for my size, so I'd stock up on the chops and cheese and chocolate, mostly.

I'd change the sheets on the most comfortable bed, check my pistols, set up my little gas heater, and hope I was too tired to dream. Sometimes, if there was a wood stove, I'd kindle a small fire. I always had a good supply of candles, so I used the miners' lamp sparingly. Sometimes it was a little spooky and it was never quite what I'd call cozy. It was just how I got along.

". . . a strange vibe."

Zak, *or Zelda*, and Andy would have had Mom come in through the front door, surely, not the unlocked upstairs window.

Foregoing my usual operation, I went straight downstairs, being careful not to slip in the snow I'd kicked in. I rounded the rail where it came into the front rooms–a large diningroom, which opened on one side to the kitchen, and on the other to a small livingroom.

A door led further back into the house, off the wall with the large bookshelf. I turned the lamp up to setting three, and slowly swept the three rooms that I could see. A scorched smell hung in the frigid air but the place looked otherwise fine, as if the owners had just stepped out. I brought the beam to rest on the front door. Taped to the inside of the bulging window was a paper, *probably a note from Zak.*

I walked over and pulled the scrap of paper free from the glass. It told Mom to look for the house key "the same place we keep ours," and for her to come in and wait for them–that they would be back soon. The note was from Andy and Ztephen. *Ztephen? I stand corrected. Good to meet ya I'm sure.*

I turned around and quickly swept the livingroom to my right, and the diningroom, left. Across from me was the door to the back end of the house. A card was taped to that door.

The card held another message, "Mom–second door on right. Andy." I pulled the card and flipped it over. It was Andy's business card.

BREEZ PRODUCTIONS
ANDY BREEZ–VIDEOGRAPHER
From Ads to ZZoom-3D
We do Weddings–Affordable!
Satisfaction Guaranteed

On the bottom of the card was his contact info. *All useless now.*

The scorched smell was like a physical presence in the livingroom. I turned, sweeping the darkness from ceiling to floor. From this vantage point I could see the farthest corner clearly but I flipped the lamp up to four, for just a few seconds–the widest beam with the most candle power.

Large windows lined the two outside walls. A plush wraparound couch also filled that corner. The window curtains were gone. One of the rods still hung crookedly from one of its brackets. There was a haphazard heap of curtains and blankets at the corner of the couch, spilling off onto the floor.

At first it had seemed tidy and ordinary–nice enough–but with splashes of chaos at the corners. Light danced crazily off the windows, filling the area with glaring reflections and oddly cut shadows as I scanned the room.

Snow was piled tight up over the windows outside–enough so that the weight of it had cracked one of the outside storm windows and the glass was pressing heavily on the inner pane. Between the sparkling of snow and the kaleidoscope of reflections, it took a minute to take in the story this room was telling. But it was a message I'd seen too many times over the last couple months.

Something, *or someone*, had caught fire here, a small fire in this case, and somebody had been around to put it out. It looked like there had been a moment of pandemonium in an otherwise ordered life. Hastily filled pans of water were thrown, magazines strewn, and burning items smothered under blankets. The glass coffee table was cracked and littered with sooty ashes. Part of the glass was heat warped. There was also the faint white powder indicative of a type 'C' fire extinguisher.

I spent just a few more minutes poking through the livingroom. Absent from the burned area were any traces of human remains. Someone had cleaned it up a little I guessed. Sometimes I found teeth and a few shards of blackened bone, as well as metal items such as buttons, zippers, buckles, glasses, watches, cell phone blobs, and so on.

I decided to follow Andy's directions, and go down the back hall to the second door to the right. I found myself leading the way with my hammer. *I'm just creeping myself out now.*

I knew the place was vacant–had been since shortly after El Vaca obviously–but every one of these places where I came upon the fire spots, had a strange vibe. Something other than the smell lingered on. I had in fact, been tending to avoid them more lately as a place to spend the night, and at the same time finding more of them.

I pushed the door open and peered through. The miner's headlamp flooded the length of the hallway. I always had the hammer on these missions, and there was always some practical task for it. But for now, I slipped it back into its loop, with a casual twist.

Mom,

I wanted to write this, just in case. We're waiting here for you. If you're not here when I finish this, I'm coming to look for you. I love you Mom. I want you to know that. I don't say it ~~enouf~~ enough, and I fight with you too much and I don't do like you want me to. I'll do better tho. I hope you get this note if I don't make it thru, if I Flame Out like Andy's roommate and the others, while I'm coming up to get you.

I hope your not mad at me for taking Grampa's old truck. Andy needed my help this morning, and they called off school after you went to work. We got some great vids of the comet, but then everything went haywire, and all the news was about ~~peices~~ pieces of it coming down. Everyone was running, and driving crazy. But not us. The cops was telling us to get to cover, Andy just told them we was with the news. Then the cops went flame-on too.

Love Ztephen

Flame Out . . . Flame-on? Confused, I put the handwritten note aside. There were several more beneath it. I hoped they were more legible than the last. *She never saw these then.*

Dearest Mother,

How can I put into words my horror and confusion over today's events? And now what is to come after the comet, and after all the people bursting into flames? [Words deeply scribbled out] I have to believe it happened the same everywhere else. Now with winter here, and the electric down everywhere, it won't be long and everything about our old lives will be gone!

The few people that are left are mostly bent on heading south before Christmas. We'll be going too. Hexiss maybe, Aunt June's.

We'll decide in the morning. Ztephen is sleeping, finally.

I stayed up to edit the recordings I got earlier. They may be important someday. Thank you for everything. I expect to get the chance to tell you that, face to face. I'd better get some sleep now myself, if I can manage.

Love, Andy

There were a few pages more in several entries, detailing the things they had done and seen after the comet. The boys had stayed around town for two more days, helping the few other survivors, planning, and packing. Ztephen had insisted on going back one more time to look for his mother. He'd picked up Perry, a young friend from his neighborhood who had lost his home, and his entire family to the engulfing green flames. Together they had left the painted messages I'd come across.

The following morning the three had left, headed for Hexiss, taking the old pickup, since it happened to be one of the few things that still worked by then.

Andy had left a flash drive marked '12-21-2112' next to the notes for Mom, but I couldn't get the one remaining computer to boot-up with the power left in the backup.

Around Andy's workroom, a few odd pieces of equipment were strewn on the tables–things a Videographer might leave behind, considering the situation. Eventually I found one older vid-cam that I was able to cobble together with a couple spare items, to replay the contents of the flash drive.

A young man's face filled the tiny screen. "I'm Andy Breez, and what you're about to see . . ." he began in a serious tone. Andy was a handsome man, but my attention was completely taken by the haunted look in his eyes. ". . . to say that the comet was BIG, is to say the least," he went on. "When I first saw El Vaca, I had the irrational but unshakeable thought that it was a divine messenger from the sky. God himself maybe."

He went on to reiterate a lot of what I'd already heard on the radio that fateful day. The white background behind him meanwhile faded into a scene of blue-green sky, with winter's high clouds. At the edge of the screen, burning brilliantly across the sky, was the comet. It had already come as close it was going to, and was miraculously headed back to the heavens. I felt like cheering, but as it climbed on its tail of brimstone and ash, the sky began to rain fire.

The battery pack burned up before the recording finished, so I stashed the rest of the setup in my pack, with the hope of finding power for it later.

MAMAS AND THE PAPAS

Mid May. Almost to the Gulf of Kalexico.

Most of my early traveling had been on skis, following the power lines south along major highways. Then, in the state of Mariahbronn, I'd played the hunch that I would find the Hexarkana unfrozen, navigable, and that had gotten me from there to the Narcissippi.

The going by boat had been slower than skis at first. The river had been anemic then. Sometimes there was ice halfway across the channel, and I was new to pulling the oars. However, after the first couple of days on the water, I was making as much southbound progress as I would have on the skis, more when I could coax a bit of life out of the old MuckRaker.

The Jackson had finally died on me for good, but I didn't mind the quiet. I did keep one eye peeled for something better to replace it though. I could not have still skied very well even if I had wanted to, so I paddled.

Tuva would have had some special Ivik-Tuvic word for this kind of snow; *Igardgooksuk, or some such thing.* It was hard-packed, icy and gritty, dangerous for skiing except on the flats. Strap on metal cleats, to my boots if needed, and I could easily enough run on it in the mornings when the crust was still frozen. As each new day progressed, and the feeble light cut through the enveloping but ever thinning high-borne dust, there would often be enough warmth to turn it all to slush.

I was glad for the boat because, even though the river could be treacherous, 'igardgooksuk' could break your bones, and hip deep slush is to skiing what 'greased' is to pig catching.

At that time, there was still some hope of making my way southeast to the big river, then due south, then east again on highway forty-three, eventually to reach Blakely and any of my family there, if they still lived. They didn't though–I became surer each day. If they did, they too would head down to the coast.

There didn't seem to be *anyone* left, dead or alive. Granted, I didn't spend a lot of time looking, beyond what I could see from the river. I hadn't seen recent traces of human life anywhere–plenty of confused and pathetic looking critters though. I was going to be on this journey for up to another month before I made it to the southern coast, where there would surely be throngs of survivors.

Meanwhile I would press on, with care, and as much speed as the river allowed. *And if I do find someone, what then? What if they're the unscrupulous type?*

Sometimes I'd actually catch myself acting out this whole scene, practicing like in boot camp, going through the deadly motions, mostly to stay sharp, but in part for my own amusement.

"Hello Mr. Thugly," I'd say to a willing tree trunk. "How you likin' this lovely weather? Oh by the way–I might look like a cold and lonely little brown sugar, but you'll just be keeping that boner in-house *moh'fo*," by which time I'd have my skinning knife at his throat, Ol' Snub drawn and trained on his 'third eye' while I continued, "cause I'm one bad-ass bitch!"

Just about then, Thugly's good old buddies would come stepping out from behind a fence or another big tree. A quick deep slice and 'K'pow', a short dodge and run, a leap and roll, another two shots, and there would be three pretend corpses at my feet.

Then I'd spend the next ten minutes feeling silly, shaming myself for such cynicism.

Night was settling in early when I pulled up to the nearly submerged yet extravagant dock. I climbed out and hauled the boat up to shore where I heaved it out onto dry land. A short way inland was my objective.

It was one of *those* houses. When the floodplain extended out too far for most people to put their houses on the river's edge, the rich simply engineered what looked like a reverse moat. They built a berm of aerth, about three meters high in this case, all the way around the house and barns. Since the waters were already rising, this place would once again be a small square island. I of course would be long gone by then.

When the flood came, it would surely be of historic proportions. By morning, I expected to find the river risen by another hand-span or so. Another week though, I estimated, and I would be far from here, making my home in a nice place on the coast of the gulf, becoming part of a new community–*the few, the proud, the refugees.* Two weeks beyond that, and I would at least try to have something of a garden started. This place, by then, would have water over halfway up its causeways.

It had been several years since I'd put a hoe in the ground. I had my first real garden the year my father had his last. His took up half the back yard, which wasn't so uncommon in our poor neighborhood. The government would provide seeds, tools, education, and even help, for those in need, and able to help themselves.

Papa had a garden even before that though. He did it because he enjoyed it. I had wanted to try it too, mostly to be close to him. I didn't know it wouldn't be forever, or that those long gone times would become my most cherished memories of him.

Looking at this place, momentarily reminded me of my little garden plot, and not because there were signs of a fenced-in kitchen garden between the southwest corner of the berm and the house. The connection came from the fact that my father had affectionately called my little nook of the garden, 'Wilhelmina's postage stamp'. I imagined this place from the air a month in the future, with water all around it, like a giant postage stamp commemorating the end of the world winter of twenty-one-twelve, on a giant envelope of water.

It was getting dark. I had to stop thinking about the good things that went bad, which at this point was everything. I had work to do here. Even with the good currents I'd hit, it had already been a long day, at a little less than fifty kilometers.

The place was locked up tight. It was just a matter of figuring out which window to take out. I decided on the one next to the door of course like I'd seen in the movies, so I could reach in to unlock the deadbolt.

I stepped in over the shards of glass. The place had the hint of a musky odor that I couldn't place, and the faint scorched scent that I had become used to. At least it didn't give the immediate impression of having been looted, for some reason.

I was finding more and more places that were either burned to the ground or broken into, the farther south I traveled. I considered the break-ins a good sign, in one respect. It had made me a bit paranoid though, until I reminded myself that, until I actually met someone, I couldn't prejudge the situation.

Another factor had figured itself in however as of a few days prior, one that had wrapped the sinister promise of gruesome death about it. I'd come across a place, nice enough from the outside, but that had been busted into and senselessly vandalized, especially in the kitchen. I moved on quickly to another house from there, but that night, I awoke from a dream of myself tearing up the place in which I was then staying.

In the dream I'd caught an unsettling glimpse of myself in the living room mirror as I hurled the coffee table through the sliding glass door. I stopped and looked back into the mirror in horror at what I thought I'd seen. I'd been about to smash the mirror too, when I woke up.

The dream abruptly shattered like the slider. I shot upright in the strange bedroom, quelling sounds of breaking glass and images of burning eyes, *my eyes*, beneath unkempt brown fur.

With my fingers wrapped around Midnight's cold stock beneath the pillow, one snaking its way around the trigger, I listened intently, not daring even to think, as several tense minutes dragged by, and no sounds came. I had earlier, as usual, strung a few simple booby traps about the place. I might have heard something in my sleep, and whatever it was, my subconscious had passed it into my dreaming, warping it. *Maybe so, maybe not.*

I began to put together as much of the dream as I could remember–by the time I was done, I'd come to the conclusion that the kitchen in the previous place had been ransacked in the simple quest of an overdue spring bear, in her hunger, a plight I could sympathize with. The dream had just been a warning, not so urgent, not about my fellow human refugees–if indeed there were any–but about migrating grizzlies.

Or was it about your own inner nature? The question brought me back to the present, and the work ahead. *I've really got to quit talking to myself. I'll end up with a bucket of possums in one hand, and a pail of piss in the other.*

Anyway, when I saw this house, the berm, it said money–a nice place then. It even looked as if some fool thought he'd come back here. It had been tidied up. The sheets were clean. Much of the food had been packed off apparently, but that was fine. I could get comfortable here, if for only a night.

I looked out into the night. My ghostly reflection in the bedroom windowpane was candle lit–I struck the pose of a body builder. *Not bad for a girl. I'd do me.*

I laughed out loud at my own joke, but then I thought more seriously about how wound-up I really was. *'Wound-up'* was a phrase my Aunt Sophie always used when she talked about Mama . . . *Like an eight-day clock, lookin' for co—*

I heard a muffled clunking downstairs! I quicky wetted the fingertips of both hands with spit, and simultaneously snuffed out both candles. I was sure the sound hadn't come from any of my strung-up noisemakers. I'd locked the place up tight–even nailed a scrap of plywood over the broken window beside the front door. The sound had definitely come from inside though.

I heard it again.

Then I let out a relieved breath, realizing that it had been nothing more than firewood settling in the stove in the room below.

I looked out the window, with eyes now adjusted to the dark. A high flung half moon barely lit the unaerthly landscape. If it wasn't for the lingering fields of dimly glittering hard-packed snow, I wouldn't have seen a thing beyond the bermed yard. I could just see the spot where I'd pulled up the rowboat. I was trying to focus in on its shape when I saw a hulking black figure moving near it, slowly but surely.

So far, the odorous peppery powder that people sprinkled around their trash bins to ward off nocturnal gremlins–draccoons, and other such critters–had served well for the coyotes and wolves. It was something I had started doing up north on a hunch when I first came across a canister of the stuff in a sporting goods store. At twelve dollars and ninety-five cents a shot, but free to me, I couldn't pass it up.

My new tactic however, was to bring in the food and sprinkle the deterrent around outside the house.

I knelt down at the window and put my head to the glass to watch. With some satisfaction, I realized that it was a bear, and that it would find nothing worth tearing into the boat for, as I had earlier sledded the tote full of food up to the house. I had started this practice two nights ago, after the warning dream. *Might as well get comfy.* I rested my elbows on the wide sill and tilted my head so as not to steam up the glass. For a while she didn't do much more than pad sluggishly along the water's edge, forth and back, forth and back. I was interested to see if it would follow the scent of the food to the house, and if the powder would persuade it to move off.

I'd been considering upgrading my fire power. Here was a prime reason. I could easily slide the window open and rest a rifle–night-scope equipped–on the sill and take the bear out with a single shot, if need be. *Tack it to the wall soldier. That's what I'm talking 'bout.*

The big old animal hoisted itself up onto its haunches, almost leaning backwards as it sat there testing the air with its big old nose. *She smells something, sure'nough.*

I shouldn't even be here! By now I should be on the Delta. I had been telling myself for a week that I was wasting my time paddling that damned boat. I was on the outskirts of Bedford, a sizeable river-town. One way or another I'd be leaving Bedford with a new boat. I had already thought of putting in the effort to equip the old rowboat with a new motor–the old Muck-Raker was its anchor! But I needed something different, better. And why not go for the gold. The river's depth and width allowed for some pretty damn big boats; even all the way up to the Olympian Lakes. *And Marian Evans,* a long lost up-north friend. *Probably gone like everyone else.*

I could sleep on the new boat, eat, drink, pee, and play solitaire too. With a big motorboat I could use the time and energy I would save, by stopping to gather anything I might need in my new life, and have all the more room to gather that much more.

I was just starting to make a mental list of the things I would look for–my mind was brimming with necessities and possibilities–when old Mother Bear started padding back toward the rowboat. Before I knew it, she was climbing in.

I'd been getting ready for bed. I still had my snow pants on, but it had warmed up enough in the house to get down to a long sleeved thermal on top. I was used to sleeping with one or two layers of clothes, and as many blankets as I could pile on comfortably. I had never actually seen a bear up close, and realized with some amazement that this long feared encounter was going to take place now and here, of all places. I pulled my jacket on in the dark, cursing under my breath with as much good humor as I could manage.

Jacques had made a few applicable matter-of-fact chicken scratch entries in his log book–tales of his encounters with grizzlies. Hardly a year of his nineteen at the mine had gone by without at least one. He'd always been able to scare off the intruder with loud noises. It was part of his job. And Martin had of course explained what he called 'Bestial Politiques'.

Have I got a surprise for you old girl!

On my way out, I stopped at the bathroom for a couple cotton balls, and stuffed them in my ears.

I took the most direct route–out the back door and straight up the side of the berm, digging in my boot toes for purchase in the hard snow. This part of the earthwork was actually bare on top down to the brown grass. I was across the width of it in two strides, and she was in view. I hesitated for a moment before digging my heels as quietly as I could into the side facing the river. I held Midnight before me, cocked. Mother Bear was sitting in the bottom of the boat, gnawing on something.

It was the port-side paddle!

She lowered the oar as she raised her head in my direction. I could hear her masticating the leather covering she'd peeled off the paddle handle. I took deliberate steps diagonally down the ridge.

She dropped to all fours and stepped out of the boat in one fluid motion. I gave her two seconds to head either left or right, but she came straight for me. I shouted and waved my arms and jumped up and down for about two more seconds but she kept coming, moving faster.

Have it your own way then bitch. I flipped the lid on Jacques' old lighter and lit it as I wedged it between my left thumb and the handgrip of the .38-caliber. I dug into my right-hand coat pocket and pulled out two of the little charges I'd hauled since the mine, lit them and tossed them in quick succession to land between us.

I dropped to the snow and rolled my face away from the blasts. When the first one went off, it should have been anywhere between four and six meters in front of her and a bit to her left. I held my position, assuming that she would have at least stopped in her tracks. The second blast came. I'd been careful to toss it to a spot to her right and a bit further in front of her, so that the blast from the first one couldn't push the second one my way.

I stuffed the lighter back into my pocket as I rolled to a sitting position. I hadn't seen the flashes, so my eyes were still accustomed to the dark, but in my mind's eye Mama Bear was running away, not standing defiantly, a full three meters tall.

She let out a dismissive angry grunt as she fell to her front paws. She shook her ponderous head as if to try to talk herself out of the lesson she was about to teach me. I heard the tinkling of bells. She shook her head again, and again the bells.

What the?!

I started backing toward the berm, as she slowly took a few heavy steps in my direction. My best shot would be from a higher angle so I turned and darted up. She was coming faster when I wheeled around! I took six calm quick shots as she continued to pick up speed. She finally tumbled like a train wreck and slid several meters, actually bouncing off the berm with enough force that the ground quivered beneath me.

It had taken each of the five slugs that hit her, passing through a small circle on her thick shoulders, to bring her down. I rolled her limp body over with some effort, enough to see her chest and belly, and was amazed to see that only one slug had passed clean through. The rest had hit bone, mushroomed, fractured, and filled her chest with little explosions of lead.

She had come on, a snarling juggernaut, until the very last shot had severed her spine taking her back legs out of commission. I pulled the cotton balls from my ears and flicked them to the wind.

Someone had collared her, and the collar had a transmitter and a sturdy set of silver tags. *Not bells then.* The smell of her kept me from examining too closely.

I'd seen some close fighting in my days up north, but it always left me shaken. Sleep would be a hard won goal but it was really what I needed. I would get a look at those tags and see to the boat in the morning.

A warmish breeze was starting to come up from the south. As I crested the berm I stopped to feel it on my face, imagining I could smell the faintest trace of sea air. I was sweating in the heavy clothes, so I took off my hat and let the breeze lift my hair and it helped to calm me. I stood for a while trying to recall the few good memories held in my mind's back pocket.

I remembered my father and our siamese twin gardens. Remembered Tuva–the something we had that wasn't a lover's lullaby, but was in some ways, just as close. And I remembered the sights I'd seen in the great wide North. Nature in her unblemished beauty, to me had become glorious beyond all of man's creations.

It was some minutes later that I realized I was on my knees, sobbing to the moon as she slowly sank toward the west. A fire in my soul was stirring. A strange hypnotizing image formed in my mind of a giant man of stacked stone, pointing out my way for me. Then something came to my ear from the direction of the house.

"Lightning gave the titanic statue the illusion of movement."

It was a clunking sound like I'd heard before. But this, I knew, was not the settling of firewood in the stove.

I reloaded the .38 from the box in my top pocket. I still had a couple of the mini-sticks in my coat. I stuffed my hat into my inside pocket, and heel stepped down the bank toward the house.

When I'd first found this place, I'd given it my usual once over, but saw now with my flashlight, the low hidden entrance behind the overgrown juniper. It led into a crawl space, no doubt.

I'd been too focused earlier on getting through the front door. I'd overlooked this seldom used entry. I pulled the evergreen fronds back to reveal a little door that had been forced open. Claw marks betrayed the intruder. I leaned in closer–there was the thick pungency I'd smelled on Mama bear. There also was the single bell-like jingle of another set of tags, on another collar, *Baby Bear? Of course. Or Papa maybe . . . Should have known there would be a crawl space, as high as the house sits.*

I backed out of the bush slowly. "Grizzlies go for the skull," Martin had said, "or anywhere they can sink their teeth in that's convenient. But they like to gnaw their way around your head, until they get it to crack a little, then viola!"

He had been trying to talk me into the bigger gun, his .45, after I'd agreed to stay on at the mine last fall. I had declined on the basis that Jacques' .38s fit me better, and that I did have larger calibers in the two rifles over the door. Besides, I knew from past experience how many more rounds I could get into a moving target with a smaller piece.

I shown the light down. The snow was unmarked beneath my feet. The south winds actually had the temperature rising now, but it had been chilly all day, and the snow was still like concrete. I moved back and around the corner, walking faster until I reached the back porch. The screen door was ajar as I had left it.

I tiptoed down the central hall to where it opened up at the front of the house to the large area which combined livingroom, diningroom, and kitchen. I stepped out of the hall onto a circular throw rug. Beneath me the floor creaked slightly.

I pulled the rug aside. *A trap door!* It was latched, but I took no comfort from the little mechanism. I was sure that the grizzly, if it wanted to, could chew its way up through the floor. More realistically though, I envisioned it coming out of the crawlspace the way it had gotten in, and then busting through any of the windows or doors.

I pulled the rug back over the trapdoor and shown the light across the room to the little red sled I'd pulled into the house. It had my tote full of food strapped to it.

I pulled the sled to the hallway, hating the way it scraped loudly over the floor. I undid the bungees and lifted the tote, testing the weight. I didn't think I could carry it *and* the pack the whole distance, so I strapped it back down. I moved it onto the throw rug, and silently slid the rug and all, the rest of the way to the back of the house.

The hall opened on my right to a cozy little sitting room where the old Franklin cooked merrily along. I dodged up the stairway to the room I had staked out for the night, skipped over the trip wire, and rounded the corner into the bedroom. The only thing I needed sat on the bed–I'd already finished repacking it.

I slung the pack up and around behind me, squirming into its straps as quick as I could in the dark. There was a faint clump-scrape-jingling sound from below as I made my way back to the top landing.

I side stepped down and quietly into the sitting room where my gloves were drying by the fire. I stuffed them down the front of my coat. At the back door I considered the miner's lamp. I'd earlier left it hanging there on a peg after getting old Ben fired up.

I heard something from outside the back door. *Damn, Damn, and Damn.*

A two minute dash could have put me safely at the riverside. *I'll leave the food Papa Bear. You can have it all. I can resupply tomorrow.* Bedford would surely provide both a new boat and a new tote, and fill the tote with frozen steaks and shrimp, whatever I wanted. I started to form a plan. I would quietly remove the tote's lid and start chucking the food out the front door. That would attract the big fella, and allow my escape.

The back porch's outer screen door rattled. I peered out through the inner door, through the porch, and saw the bear sniffing all around the jamb. He was half standing, on the back steps, but instead of coming through the flimsy door, he dropped and deftly backed down off the steps. I sensed he was heading around to the east side of the house.

I followed his leisurely progress around to the front of the house by tip-toeing from room to room, window to window. As he came up on the front porch, I was standing in the middle of the front room, Ol' Snub in one hand, Midnight in the other.

After awhile he retreated from the door, but I could have sworn he tested to see if the doorknob would turn. *Taste testing maybe? Well, I wonder what he thinks about Varmit-B-Gone.*

I crept to the front wall of windows and pulled the curtain back a bit. He was up on the southeast corner of the berm, silhouetted against the moonlit sky. I wondered if he was going to wander off–hoping so–when I saw my break.

He was crouched in an odd position, which I realized was his stance for doing what all bears are known for doing in the woods. I hoped he had a whole winter's worth of it, and that he would be constipated about it.

I dashed back down the hall as fast as I could with the heavy pack on my back, and looped the sled's rope around my wrist. I was careful going down the back steps so the sled wouldn't topple, then hit the snow running.

I dashed immediately to the right for the long causeway that would make it easier to get up and over the berm with the sled. The sled kept trying to run me over going down the outer causeway. That and a sudden animal panic drove me forth in a reckless dash. I made it to the boat without slipping on the hard-pack, just as a thick cloud was blotting out the moon.

I was sweating and out of breath, but hoisted the tote, sled and all, up into the back. The boat was easy enough to push into the water–high on adrenalin as I was–the trick was to keep it from floating away as I peeled the pack off, and tossed it into the back also.

I had forgotten the miner's lamp! A momentary sense of nostalgia, and lapse of reason, had me backing away from the boat for a second. I had other light sources. And I needed one badly, as I realized that one oar was missing, gone from its socket.

I turned to look for the oar as I sought to fish the flashlight out of my big left pocket. My hand instead found Midnight's pommel. I pulled the gun, to switch pockets, but its sight caught on the cloth, causing it to flip out of my hands. I juggled the thing several times in the dark, before funneling it between my breasts, against my pounding heart.

I could now hear the heavy scrabble of claws on ice, and a panting sound like winds in a canyon, rushing toward me from up the bank. I cocked the weapon and fired, until it was emptied into the advancing shadow.

ADELLE AND THE JUMP-OFF

"And that's the last thing I remember," I said, "until I woke up here."

I looked around me at the rapt round faces, and realized without thinking, that I had a once in a lifetime opportunity. I threw my arms out, making claws of my hands, and jumped forward with the biggest roar I could muster. A few of the kids fell for it, and scattered, screaming into the water, until our laughter brought them back to the benches. My smile lingered, but my mind leapt ahead to the certainty that the ones who had run were not right for what I had in mind–a voyage back to the northern continent–they were too young yet, but neither was this the right time to broach the subject with those who might be up to it. I was exhausted.

"I tried later to figure out how many days I was afloat. I don't remember anything coherent after the fight, but I do know that neither of my canteens leaked, and that I'd just filled them both, but when I awoke on Adera, the one beside me was empty. Don't know how fast I would have traveled but, we do know Adera lies out from the delta about ninety kilometers."

"Just beyond the northern horizon," said Ardonna thoughtfully, looking out over the bay.

"I heard you can see it from the top of Lac Syph," added Vouy, the youngest of the bunch at ten years old, and the most outspoken.

Vouy's older brother stood up, stretching his lanky youthful body, and turned to look at the dunes several hundred meters behind us. From this angle, we could just see the place at the top where I had come ashore. "What happened to all the stuff you brought? You said you got paid in gold–you wouldn't have left that behind," he said.

"Had it stashed beneath the sirloins. I still have some of it, just a keepsake really."

"And you said you took, *looted,* what you wanted along the way," began Meera, "as would I–but what sorts of things? There must have been a million things you could have taken."

"Nothing much of any real importance now that I think back . . ." I was thinking of one thing though, the vid-cam–Andy's recordings of El Vaca, when the people of Echo stood and burned. I'd presented it to the elders years ago. I was too drained now to go into it though. We all needed to stretch our legs.

"Shall we go down to the jump-off?" It had been a long spell of sitting, and the agreement was *almost* unanimous. I too began looking forward to a brisk swim.

"I have a bad feeling," said Vouy.

"So do I," said Meera, wringing her hands.

I'd wanted to go along with them this time, if only to satisfy my curiosity about something strange I'd seen out on the water, coming to shore in that direction, but if anyone had learned to trust intuition, I had. "We won't go then. What shall we do inst—?"

"We have to! It'll be worse if we don't," said Meera.

I glanced around from one expectant face to the next, undecided. *It's just the story–the fight with the bear–still spooks me too.* "By all means then, let's go," I said, and looked to see if we were all ready.

There was one part of the trail that veered inland a bit where a small pie-shaped piece of land was missing, eroded away, it made a beautiful little inlet which ended at a small waterfall. The trail went up over the waterfall across a small foot bridge, and then back down to the jump-off.

From the bridge we could see the top of a small square blue-green sail on the far side of the rock. I'd noted it coming in an hour earlier, during a barrage of questions about why a bear would have a collar. It wasn't like the sails I was used to seeing, but I hadn't given it much regard. I'd seen it from quite a distance after all, but from the bridge, I could see it was definitely not Aderan.

"something strange I'd seen out on the water"

"Stop," I said to the children just behind me, who were babbling all at once that we should 'run on down there and see what's going on'.

"I'll go. You will stay here. If I motion like this," I made a hearty overhead wave of my hands, "or if anything looks fishy, make a call for help, and then head for the chapel—if no one's there, keep going, find Harmyn."

I waited two milliseconds for an answer. "Got it!?" I insisted. A few of them nodded. "Good!"

I started down the path, but turned back after a few steps and put my finger to my lips, for good measure. They nodded as one in comprehension. The trail sloped away steeply from there, and I started jogging down in long strides.

I made it out onto the jump-off and slowed down to a walk when I could again see the top of the sail. I was about to stop to try to think of what to say, if this was indeed what I thought it was. I started going through a few phrases of welcome in English. Then my heart sank as I heard the first few desperate shouts.

I began taking small unconscious steps toward the edge. I had a good idea what was happening when the screaming came.

I could hear two voices. A woman was screeching incoherently, and a man was howling obscenities. His voice was pained and desperate, and muffled through half drowned coughs. It was a shark attack!

I sprinted across the rest of the rock in seconds, and the strange craft came into view anchored just beyond the ledge. It looked like two pontoon boats craftily lashed together lengthwise. I slowed down as the rest of the scene sank in.

Immediately I was thrown into the frantic realization that I was unarmed, except for the knife I still carried. Not that my old .38s would be of much use in this situation, but the Aderans had weapons that worked selectively to exclude humans from their damage.

I looked down to see a young couple flailing away from a pair of sharks. Luckily the sharks were small, and they weren't coordinating their attacks. The man was kicking at one shark while the other circled wide. Blood streamed from his leg, turning the water red. The girl was trying to dog-paddle to the makeshift houseboat.

I watched in shock as the wide shark came in with a sudden powerful lunge, I could see it clearly as it slammed the girl's chest and passed by to circle again. She fought for breath, screamed, and stopped swimming for the boat.

I turned to the children still on the bridge and waved to them as we'd arranged. They turned in unison and ran back down the path for help, all but Meera–she was already dashing toward me. I didn't have time to think about how I would later address her disobedience.

The man was having a bad time with his shark.

Wide shark was starting another run. I knew its tactic from my training with Xoqueicue. It wanted to stun the girl, so it could then rend her to gulpable sized pieces.

If I took time to use the comring, they could both be dead before help arrived, so I pulled my old knife and backed up several paces. I ran forth and launched myself over the edge, taking a deep breath, arching into the long dive.

I hit the water cleanly and went deep before powering back up, underneath the girl, just in time to see the shark darting toward her. Apparently it was as intent on hitting her with one last good blow, as I was upon gutting it.

I brought the blade up just as the gruesome jaws passed over in a blur. Its innards spewed forth even as it hit the girl again, knocking the wind out of her. She tumbled in the water like a doll in a washing machine.

I came up for air. There was no sign of the man, or the sharks. Again I dived, in the girl's direction. I saw her going down, bubbles streaming from her lips, her long blonde hair like streamers in an updraft.

I was finally able to get hold of her limp hand. *Can't save her!* I stifled the thought of defeat, for the moment. We almost made it back up to the sun, and air, before I saw a dark figure swimming toward us.

I was on the verge of blacking out, and had to let go of her wrist to swim up for another breath. My heart was hammering at my ribs, my lungs burning for oxygen.

I made the surface, gasped in several deep breaths, and was about to make another dive for her, when the water erupted next to me. It was our brave young Meera. Savior Meera. She had the other girl in her arms.

Together we got her to the safety of the boat.

"Harth was more of a large sprawling village than any city."

"To the east was the tower called Lac Syph."

EPILOGUE–RAINBOWS AND PROMISES

The cheery sweet sounds of a wredren filter through the window of my waking mind. Little Tuva is snuggled to my breast. He's still asleep, starting to stir. I lazily stretch as much as I can without disturbing him, he would wake up looking for something I couldn't give. I let my arm fall to the left side of the bed–the spot is cold.

Xoqueicue must have arisen early. I feel the warm echo of his kiss on my temple, and in my heart. I scoot my butt backwards expecting to bump into Adelle but that side is cold also.

The baby squirms against me. I cup his beautiful bulbous head in my hand, stroke his silky straw-colored hair. It's been a year since Adelle and her brother came to the island, a year since her brother's horrible death at the jump-off. How things have changed since then.

After Adelle was rushed off to the healers at Lac Syph, and the children were returned home safely, I went to find Xoqueicue. In the trauma of that day, something in me had snapped.

I remember being in such an odd state; scared, determined, in love, 'wound up' . . . and exhausted all in one. I told him something like, "If you don't kiss me right now, you're a damn fool!"

Adelle had moved in with me as soon as her wounds healed. We grieved together for her brother, though I had never known him. He must have been someone special if he was anything like her. We were like long-lost sisters. When we became lovers, it was as natural as a leaf turning toward the sun. When we invited Xoqueicue to join us, it became as glorious as a field of Hexiss sunflowers in full bloom.

And now here we are climbing the ladder of time together, and baby makes four.

Our new place is at the island's west end high up the spine, near a familiar spring with the purest water–It's a cozy little bungalow grown from stone into the east side of a familiar ridge. We've been here seven months now and it gets better every day.

I close my eyes, thinking I might just steal a few more minutes sleep. The wredren continues his tremolo-chirp-serenade outside with a gaiety that always invites me to get up early. *Not this time.*

I wake again with the baby tucked protectively beneath my arm, my nose buried in his wispy curls. He searches for and finds my nipple–I let him suckle for the moment, not out of some unfulfilled mothering instinct, I tell myself, but as a pacifier. He soon gets wise and pulls away with a betrayed whimper. I let him try my pinky finger as I swing my legs out of bed.

"Adelle?" I don't smell a breakfast. *Odd.* "Cho?"

"Well, where did those two go? It's just you and me I guess," I say to Tuva, as I lay him on the bed to change the wrap of cloth around his bottom.

I'm just finishing up when a knocking at the door startles me. We do get a few more visitors here than when it was my perch, but not many. I answer the door to find Runa with a couple bags at her feet. We hug, making a baby sandwich.

"I came a little early. Hope it's not a problem. Figured I'd take you guys with the lift–save you half a day's walk to the ship. That'll give us time to catch up on things. I've been wanting so much to see you."

"Ship?"

"You know. The Luna-wing thingy–they haven't named it yet."

"Oh yeah." I had heard about it.

"Um, I ah, I take it Cho hasn't told you yet, about any of this." She gestures at the luggage she'd brought. "*That means . . .* oh no!"

"Bring your bags in hun."

"Well, I guess it was supposed to be a surprise. Oops." She scoops up her bags and sits them just inside the door. "Maybe you can just *act* surprised?"

"I'll make us some tea, while you tell me what it is I'm not supposed to be knowing."

"Let me hold that baby, and I'll think about it."

"Yeah, actually he's hungry," I say, passing him over to the cradle of her arms. "You hold him while I try to round up Mama."

I open the side door to call for Adelle and Xoquei-cue, and see them coming down the path from the lookout. I guess they must have wanted some 'alone time' as they are both tucking here and adjusting there, and looking generally giddy.

I do my best to look surprised as we circle the western caldera, and I *am* surprised, to tell the truth. I hadn't paid much attention to any of the news about the project. I'd figured to look into it later, not that I would admit I'd lost all interest in leaving Adera, but looking down on it now I realize that I have.

Xoqueicue takes my hand. "They want you to name it," he says, with a classic dumb grin.

Again I peer down at the elegantly simple slender thing. It kinda reminds me of the enormous wind derrick rotors–blades and all–except it's hovering horizontally and has a bigger hub.

"It's really finished?" I ask as Runa takes us closer. "When do they plan to go somewhere?"

"Now," answers Xoqueicue. "They're just waiting for us to board."

"Us! All of us?"

"Adelle packed for you–the bag's stowed in the back. Runa will stay with Adelle for the ten or twelve days we'll be gone."

"Where? Where are we going?"

"Equis," he says, as if the answer should have been obvious.

"I haven't paid much attention to that sort of thing lately, I guess. I found my home." I squeeze his hand. "Refresh me on this *Equis*."

"It's another Adera," he says.

"At least it was," adds Runa, "but we haven't seen them for more than two millennia. There was no way to communicate between those of us who were hidden away in the temporal void.

"We know where they are," she continues, "we've made contact, some of us, in our dreaming, and now with radio."

Several translifts disembark from the circular topside deck as we are about to set down. "This sounds like an important expedition, why am I being allowed on?"

A crowd is forming on the deck as we climb out. Runa whispers in my ear, "you're the most important person on board, besides the captain."

Elders of the Aderan Council come forward to clasp my hands.

My mind is awash with competing thoughts and sights as we slowly spin in the giant green bowl of the blown-out old volcano. I look over the edge of the deck railing. High white clouds in a majestic sky are reflected in the deep dark little lake below. I lean out a little further and see the reflection of the ship, and myself.

The deck is about fifty meters in diameter, a drab light blue-grey like the rest of the ship. The three long triangular blades, or wings–each nearly a hundred meters in length–act as light collectors, as well as provide the main drive. I've heard that the ship has several options for powering its engines, and several types of locomotion.

Unobtrusive little recording devices, one of Harmyn's projects, hover about capturing the maiden voyage ceremony. I try to concentrate on the proceedings as I also try to think about naming this wonder.

By the time it's all over, and they ask me what name I've decided to give her, I'm speechless for a moment. It's a whole new world out there, according to Adelle, so I had considered 'Second Chance', or 'Nina-pinta-and-santa-maria', or even 'The Eagle', after the moon missions.

I had also wrestled with the idea of passing the honor on to someone else, but after all I've been through in my life I decide to go for it.

I give Xoqueicue a good pinch. "That's for not telling me about all this," I whisper.

I clear my throat and step forth, proud to be here, and terrified too. "Something went terribly wrong on our world, wrong with us, Humans. Your ancestors were the best bet that a God had to fix it. And an island was the best place to let evolution teach us, something we don't seem to want to know, that our world is our island, in space." I pause to calm myself.

"I once read in a book about a single promise, made by multiple gods, from different religions. The name of the book was On the End, but I couldn't help noticing how so much of the book was on new beginnings, after the ends.

"The book's author pointed out all the different stories from different cultures about a worldwide flood, and when he laid down the major points of each story, side by side, one promise stood out." I raise my hand high and extend my index finger. "One God-awful promise . . . Some say threat.

"The promise was seen as a rainbow, and when you think of the way a rainbow is perceived by the eye, it doesn't seem so unbelievable.

"Then I saw something on a video recording one day long long ago. It was the people of Aerda, burning, in pillars of green tongued flames, and as they burned, they stood," I throw my shoulders back and raise my eyes to the clouds, "as calm as could be, or in an unbreakable trance, looking up to the sky, like they were each looking at a flaming rainbow that only they could see.

"So, in honor of that sacred promise fulfilled, I name this great ship, Rainbow Chaser."

Everyone who is not needed below to run the ship decides to stay on the deck for the takeoff. Those who were only here for the ceremony, depart. A clear dome forms out of thin air over the wide circular platform.

The craft rises suddenly like a grasshopper. There is no g-force somehow, but we are arcing eastward above the highest clouds in minutes. Then we come back down to slowly circle the wondrous city of Harth, just inside the rim of the caldera. We can see the people waving from their rooftops, and we wave back.

We make a second pass and circle the great glittering tower of Lac Syph in a close dance. As the sunset is captured by the tower's giant hanging crystal and reflected in red splashes across our deck, I am coming to realize just how beautiful and good life can be.

The sun is going down as we hop back up into the clouds and begin to chase the sunset. To my amazement we are slowly catching up to the day, and we are eventually flying under the noon sun, a position that we slow down to maintain for the sake of efficiency.

Xoqueicue and I decide to go to our quarters below to get some sleep before the back-peddling sun tries to convince us that a brand new day is upon us.

"Cho," I say as we snuggle together before sleep. "What was that the elders said earlier, about a sign, and not being able to leave the island until Adelle came?"

"I guess it was some big secret prophesy, that she had to come to Adera."

"But why her?"

"It was part of our agreement–someone from the mainland. Our ancestors had to accept a few conditions. We may not know yet exactly why we were part of the Great Spirit's plan, but we knew that if anyone had ventured off the island, more than as far as we could see, they would have been lost in the void, and that could have put all of Adera in danger."

"I mean, why not me. I came to the island from the mainland first."

"We know that now. But until Adelle came, and the green light failed to flash upon the crystal of Lac Syph on that evening, we couldn't know for sure if you really existed."

I sit up and pull his shoulder down to the bed. "You what!?!"

"Well I knew," he said.

"Well I knew too." With my eyes aflame, I bid him to continue.

"Still, until Adelle came and we were given the sign, we couldn't leave. Your arrival was different." In his eyes was a look I'd seen before from time to time, but hadn't understood until now that it was a look of reverence for me. "You were brought to Adera by the hand of a powerful spirit. The elders almost all agree that it was your teacher, Tuva. He was in you. He was also in the great stone sentinel you saw on the dunes when you came to us."

"And you were going to tell me this when?!"

"Tomorrow morning. Don't feel *too* bad though my love, for several long generations after 'the taking', my ancestors had to wonder if they themselves were indeed real. Imagine what that must have been like."

"Fine . . . but, you gotta start telling me things when you find them out. No more surprises like naming ships and such, ok?"

"Ok," he says thoughtfully. "Well, it occurs to me that you might not know this then–you get to be the first person to disembark when we get to Equis. It's kind of an honor the Elders want to give you."

"Well, you could have kept that a surprise! Honestly Cho–*sometimes* . . ."

EX POST FICTO: THE END OF THE OLD WORLD, AND THE NEW JERUSALEM

A green world, home to thinking beings, and ruled by unseen forces: so like Earth–Aerda.

Sexually conflicted, black, and a woman: the perfect antihero(?)–Willow.

Stories have a life all their own. Originally planned as a long short story, Reset took hold of me and did what it would, causing me to set aside several other projects, as it grew and grew into this little book. I'm glad it did, I enjoyed (almost) every minute of it, but it left me with the odd question of, "what to do with it?" I liked it just the way it was. I look at its brevity as one of its virtues. There's no shame in taking only as much space and time to tell a story as is necessary, quite the opposite.

What then does one do with a book–technically an over-long novella–a hair over 43,000 words? Same as with anything just outside the mainstream publishers box; let it moulder and die, self-publish, or go to the good old Vanities.

A born do-it-yer-selfer, I was led to self-publish for several reasons, artistic freedom being not the least of them. I was aware of the concept through our town's farmers' market committee, which is opting to self-publish a cookbook. Also, our family is putting together a book of my father's stories, poems, and letters, as a bit of our family lore.

Many self-published books fall into some wayward niche–a small subculture of readers prefers the novella, over any other length, for instance–and sales aren't always the driving force. They may be passionate, some are good, many are comparatively bad. Something plagues them; a lack of this, too much of that . . . .

A writer ultimately seeks to create that which will be deemed classic, maybe something Ray Bradbury's firemen would love to torch. In aiming for *timeless*-ness though, I am often aware that an equally important goal is *timeli*-ness. One without the other–while achievable and admirable–was not my idea for Reset. While I will always write to produce works aimed for my grandchildren's grandchildren, bless their unborn hearts, perhaps none will be as 'now' as is this story.

One reader described Reset as the perfect post-apocalyptic dream. We'll have to wait for Armageddon to verify that, but by then it may be too late. Another said that the only thing I should change about it is to get it published. Keeping in mind that speed is ofttimes a mix of blessing *and* curse, the quickest way I saw to do that happened to be self-publishing.

Reset was cooked up partly as 'welcome to my world', which is really Marian's world (more about her in a bit), and partly in response to the challenge to "write something better," when I complained to several people about the mildly nauseating storyline from the movie '2012'. So I started with a plausible disaster recipe, pulled a couple of old but still edible plot lines out of the brain-dump, stirred in some well aged legend, added spices, let it simmer, and here you have it.

I wrote this story, to present the Great Spirit, or God, *whoever*, as a mostly mechanistic force, ultimately unknowable, super-instinctual, neither good nor evil, functionally all-knowing and all-powerful, but *somehow* unthinking, and even unfeeling. And to hint at some of the qualities that this Great Spirit might favor in a person—in addition to the simple likelihood of their survival, in the wake of comet El Vaca—when It chooses to reset the game on one of Its living planets.

I wrote this story to poke a bit of savage fun, by comparison, at our dangerously presumptuous society, and at man's tendency toward willful and widespread forgetfulness. I wrote it to further the argument against all future war, and to advocate for some sort of planetary defense against killer comets, as a much worthier objective.

I won't apologize for use of the metric system throughout. They say the United States is the only country in the world not totally committed to adopting it, but that we encourage the voluntary use of it. I guess I have to appreciate not being forced to use one particular system over another, and I do wish that tendency toward choice might proliferate deeper into a few other areas of the government. But so few Americans use the metric system, so few volunteer. Maybe in a hundred years. If we're not all using it by then, I shudder to think why.

I mentioned the passion found in the self-publishing crowd, which is what I was talking about when I said that this story took hold of me. 'Willow' Walker, one of a few survivors of a worldwide catastrophe, comes to accept it after she finds herself stranded on the island of a technologically advanced group of descendants of the ancient Far Seers, who have come back from an alternate reality where they have dwelt for two thousand years. For me it was several months of taking another woman to bed, and watching her story unfold on the backs of my eyelids.

RESET is my first novel, several others are in early stages, and several shorter stories are going into submission stage now. Much of my writing experience comes from a year as news reporter for the Waterfront of Missaukee County, Michigan. Recent nonfiction work includes, writing newsletter articles, and producing the notes from meetings for three different organizations, one of which is a paying gig.

Yes, my name really is Cool. German immigrant ancestors adopted the spelling because they thought it would be cooler than K-u-h-l. ☺

I originally wrote and planned to publish this story using a pen name, Marian Evans, for several reasons, but decided to publish it under my own name for several others. The perceived benefits of using a pen name, compared to the real complications involved, are hard to balance. Growing up with a name like Cool, I knew it was likely that some people would think my real name a pseudonym anyway. I mostly wanted to avoid any limelight that would inevitably follow someone who writes as well as I hope to. I also wanted to avoid any controversy provokeable by the uneasy thoughts I might put on paper.

So, I created Marian, and she wrote Reset. I think she's good, if a little strange. But alas, "words weren't made for cowards," says Happy Rhodes. Heeding her advice, I must take the credit, the blame, and any fame, if people recommend this story to others.

—What's that? Umm . . . Marian asks me to note that she was NOT conceived and created by me.

Fine fine—I don't think I need to point out that (shhh) her initials *are* M.E. In return, she may be kind enough to refrain from explaining, *yet again,* that it's just as likely that she created me, and that I am but a crazy dream of hers.

Her name sounds like another writer, whose name and works are as liquid on the page, who was obliged to publish as a man, that her words might sell. I always wondered what that says about a man, which is all I meant to point out through the similarity to the late great Mary Ann Evans-Cross (one spelling). She had skill and grace with the written word that far exceeds my own.

Writing is my therapy for being human–after all, writers aren't cut from perfect cloth, so there are many things I do not know. One *more* thing I was trying to do with Reset was to answer myself the riddle; why do we have this universal fascination with doomsdays? Precognition *en masse?* Or is this morbid obsession linked by some strange dynamic to the instinct of species preservation (the granddaddy of all instinct)?

There is no real rationality behind the gut feeling that it would be a bad thing if our species ceased, at some future date. Though we would understandably prefer the end, if it is to be messy and inevitable, to come after our own, preferably natural, passing. In reading speculative tales, we experience mourning for even the implied death of humankind, even if it is presented as a billion years away. Looking to the past or the future for meaning, we may think it would be a waste of all that we think we have accomplished, or may accomplish. But would it? Really? Will we ever know?

I don't know that we have ever accomplished anything, or ever will, or if we are even meant to. We may be the meaningless byproducts of an infinite meaningless, a possibility not easy to meet head-on. The end of our own species by our own hand would then be as unimportant as all the other extinctions that we continue to cause.

Whatever the case, we are driven to bring meaning and purpose to our own lives, in part because we can't answer the big questions definitively, so we speculate on our own potential, and most of us find a reason or two to live and love, and to have hope for our species. Maybe that isn't easy, but I wouldn't wish for it to be–not because a God wouldn't grant it, nor would an infinite meaningless–but because of the obvious and simple fact that instinctual behavior is tied so intricately to survival. There seems to be reason enough in that. No matter how instinct developed in us and all other animal life, and regardless of the fact that it may exist for no more than its own sake, the will to live at least gives us the opportunity to ask the big questions. If there are unknowable answers to some, so be it.

One question leads to another and twenty, as usual, and I am not much closer to answering myself about, *why the doomsday obsession?* I will try to take what cold comfort I can from appreciating all the more, the questions I can answer. And to be thankful for, as an aspiring writer, the stories born where our reason meets our instinct.

Now it's done, but other questions remain. Like: why would the bears in the story wear collars? And, what was happening off the island with the scattered seeds of humanity? And why was there no contact with two of the other three hidden islands? And—

Wait—

Marian is telling me another story.

Gotta go!

LOVE AND APPRECIATION

Thanks to Mom for religion–to Dad, for the freedom to question it; to both of you for my life, and for your guidance and love.

To my team of beta-readers, for encouragement, but most of all for your criticisms: Amanda, Blake, Charles, Christina, Elaine, John, Julie, Karen, Larry, Liz, and Mike. Thanks again. I'm sure it wasn't easy with those early drafts.

Cover Magic: Linda Smith of Traverse City MI for the use of your painting Sunset on the Bay. I was impressed when I first saw it, stunned actually. Your work with metallic compounds can cause ghostly optical effects when viewed in different lights. I was visiting friends up north, and right there on their diningroom wall was Willow's little boat on the beach, and seagulls in a *different* sky. Photographer/Designer Elaine Edstrom, owns and loves the painting, so it became rather obvious who should do the cover design. Thank you ladies.

In the small town of Reed City MI, lives a big man, Steve Mann, a relatively unknown artist, whose natural talent I've long admired. Steve, I can't tell you how happy it made me when you agreed to do the illustrations. But, had I gone 'mainstream', would I suggest to the publisher that we use your work? Well, it's just not done that way. Their loss. I hope we can do it again soon.

Thanks to Ms. Belgowan, now Mrs. Maskill, for trying to teach us Pine River kids to write right, and for providing the spark all those years ago (through one of your homework assignments), for Willow Walker.

Thanks to Roger Peel of Luther MI for tech-help.

Thank you Karen and Christina, for your infinite patience and love. Also for all your help on this thing, past present and future.

And thank you reader. Marian says thanks too.

10353861R00088

Made in the USA
Charleston, SC
28 November 2011